The Baby on Marco Island

Scott Sisters Series – Book 2

AMY RAFFERTY

&

ROSE RYAN

Copyright © 2023 by Amy Rafferty and Rose Ryan

All rights reserved.

No part of this publication may be reproduced, stored, distributed, or transmitted in any form or by any means, including photocopying, recording, or other electronic or mechanical methods, without the prior written permission of the publisher or author. For permission requests, contact the author.

The story, all names, characters, and incidents portrayed in this production are fictitious. No identification with actual persons (living or deceased), places, buildings, and products is intended or should be inferred.

Images inside were designed using resources from canva.com and bookbrush.com

First Edition 2023

THE BEACH HOTEL ON MARCO ISLAND

Scott Sisters Series - Prequel

When the Scott family gathers on the beautiful Marco Island to celebrate their mother's 65th birthday, six sisters feign happiness in the face of their mother's "predictions" and their father's poor health. But each sister is followed by their own problems, causing a tangled mess of drama thinly veiled behind fake smiles.

Lorry's daughter blames her for the divorce between her parents.

Nicole is a cancer survivor grappling with being unable to conceive and her husband's reluctance to adopt.

Stephanie faces the anxiety of her husband wanting more children to add to their picture-perfect family.

Ashley and her husband struggle with IVF and the stress of managing a successful new restaurant together.

Hannah is overwhelmed with the plans for her wedding to her cardiologist fiancé, leaving her to brush off her family's poking and prodding.

Meanwhile, Jessica aches to finally set a wedding date with her fiancé Trent, who seems hesitant to commit.

In an emotionally charged tale of family, romance and womanhood, six sisters must wade through their complicated lives to save their family from crumbling.

DOWNLOAD FOR **FREE** ~ Click Here

AMY RAFFERTY VIP READERS

Don't want to miss out on my giveaways, competitions,

and 'hot off the press' news?

Subscribe to my email list.

It is FREE!

Click Here!

CONNECT WITH AMY RAFFERTY

Not only can you check out the latest news and deals there, you can also get an email alert each time I release my next book.

Follow me on BookBub

I always love to hear from you and get your feedback.

Email me at ~ books@amyraffertyauthor.com

Follow on Amazon ~ Amy Rafferty

Sign up for my newsletter and free gift, Here

Join my 'Amy's Friends' group on Facebook

CONNECT WITH ROSE RYAN

Sign up for my newsletter and keep up on all the latest book news,

release dates,

excerpts, monthly giveaways, and more!

Or follow me on my other socials including:

Facebook , **Instagram**, **Bookbub** , and **Goodreads**

Follow my author central page on Amazon: **Rose Ryan:**

TABLE OF CONTENTS

1. CHAPTER 1 — 1
2. CHAPTER 2 — 16
3. CHAPTER 3 — 32
4. CHAPTER 4 — 49
5. CHAPTER 5 — 68
6. CHAPTER 6 — 88
7. CHAPTER 7 — 105
8. CHAPTER 8 — 123
9. CHAPTER 9 — 138
10. EPILOGUE — 156

CONTINUE READING — 164

SCOTT SISTERS SERIES — 181

ALSO FROM AMY RAFFERTY — 182

COMING SOON FROM AMY RAFFERTY — 185

MORE BOOKS BY AMY RAFFERTY	201
AMY RAFFERTY VIP READERS	205
CONNECT WITH AMY RAFFERTY	206
CONNECT WITH ROSE RYAN	208
A NOTE FROM AMY RAFFERTY	209
A NOTE FROM ROSE RYAN	211

CHAPTER 1

The warm Florida sun hung high in the sky, casting a shimmering brilliance over Marco Island. It was the kind of day that postcards were made of, where the sea and sky melded seamlessly, and the world seemed bathed in golden light. Seated at a quaint seaside restaurant, Stephanie Victor, affectionately known as Steph, savored the view as much as her grilled shrimp salad. She felt a sense of contentment at the moment—a rare luxury in the whirlwind of her daily life.

Across the table, her younger sister, Hannah, stirred a lemon wedge into her water, her fingers dancing in the brilliant glare. With Hannah's long, dark, auburn hair and cool poise, she had the unmistakable air of a woman in control. Despite the informal lunch setting, her aura was one of elegance, the kind of presence that made everyone take notice.

Steph regarded her sister over the rim of her iced tea glass, her pale blue eyes filled with curiosity and concern. "So, this is the third surprise visit you've paid us in the space of three months." She took a sip of water. "What's going on, Han?"

Hannah offered a serene smile, her deep violet eyes holding their own secrets. "I needed a break from the Palm Beach hustle, Steph. Vincent has been swamped with surgeries, and well, you know how stressful that and my work can be."

Steph leaned back in her chair, studying her sister intently. "Is that all it is? Just a breather?"

Hannah's gaze flickered, a barely discernible hesitation in her response. "It's mainly that, but..." She let her words trail off.

Steph's brows furrowed. She knew her sister well, and these half-finished sentences clearly indicated that something else was bothering Hannah. "Hannah, you can talk to me. I'm your sister, you know."

Hannah sighed, her violet eyes holding a mixture of frustration and relief. "Alright, alright. It's not just about taking a break. Vincent and I, well, we've been having some issues lately."

Steph's heart went out to her sister. Hannah had a history of faltering on the doorstep of marriage, having gained a somewhat notorious reputation as the "runaway bride" in the Scott family. Despite her successful career as a psychiatrist, her love life had been nothing short of tumultuous. "What's going on? Are you having second thoughts again?"

Hannah shook her head, and her gaze showed genuine weariness. "It's not that. I do love Vincent. He's a wonderful man. But lately, I've been feeling somewhat suffocated with his schedule and all the stress. It's as if I'm being swallowed by this relationship."

Steph understood the dilemma. The prospect of losing her independence was daunting. "Have you talked to him about this?"

"We've had some heated discussions," Hannah admitted. "He's worried that I'm going to call off the wedding, and it's putting even more pressure on us."

Steph reached across the table, placing her hand over Hannah's. "Marriage is a partnership, sis. It's about finding that balance between love and freedom. You know that."

Hannah offered a weak smile, her eyes finally revealing the vulnerability she had been keeping hidden. "I know you're right, Steph. I just needed a breather to think things through."

Steph patted her sister's hand, offering her silent support. "Well, you're here now, and we're going to enjoy our time together. No heavy discussions today."

Hannah nodded in agreement, her features relaxing. "You're right. I came here to escape the drama, after all."

They returned to their meal, the sun-drenched coastline a soothing backdrop to their sisterly reunion. The restaurant bustled with chatter and the aroma of fresh seafood. As they savored their lunch, Steph couldn't help but feel a sense of contentment at having her sister by her side.

After lunch, they strolled back to Hannah's car. The air was warm and thick with the scent of saltwater. The brilliant cerulean of the Gulf of Mexico stretched out before them, a serene backdrop to their sisterly conversation.

As they approached the car, Steph felt an unexpected rush of dizziness, her surroundings blurring around her. Her steps faltered and her knees weakened. Her vision tunneled, and she collapsed into the passenger seat of Hannah's car just in the nick of time, her consciousness fading.

The world went black.

Steph awoke to the sterile scent of a clinic. The overhead lights were harsh, and her head throbbed with a dull ache. As her eyes adjusted to the brightness, she realized she was lying on a crisp white examination table.

Hannah sat beside her, her dark red hair a soft cascade around her worried face. "Thank goodness you're awake." She breathed a sigh of relief.

Steph's voice was hoarse. "What happened?"

Hannah offered a gentle, reassuring smile. "You fainted, Steph."

The room felt too white, too sterile. Steph blinked, struggling to understand. "Fainted? Why?"

Hannah reached for her hand. Her violet eyes filled with concern. "I'm not sure. But we're going to figure it out. The doctor is running some tests." She glanced around the room. "This small clinic is remarkably well equipped."

Steph blinked, the stark whiteness of the room sending a chill down her spine. Her head was heavy, and her thoughts scattered like leaves in the wind. Hannah's words swirled in her mind, and she fought to comprehend them.

The room's clinical sterility contrasted with the warmth and brightness of the day outside. She tried to sit up, but dizziness washed over her like a crashing wave. The hospital bed felt alien, unfamiliar. The fluorescent lights stung her eyes, and the sterile aroma intensified her discomfort. Hannah's violet eyes held worry and care.

"What kind of tests?" Steph asked as she tried to make sense of her surroundings. She had no recollection of how she ended up here, her mind clouded by the disorienting moment of her collapse.

"The doctor drew some blood and asked me a whole lot of questions." Hannah grinned and patted Steph's arm. "Don't worry. He's sure it's just the heat and maybe the shellfish you had for lunch."

"I have food poisoning?" Steph frowned and allowed Hannah to help her into a sitting position.

"Could be." Hannah nodded and pulled a face. "I'm sorry. I know you wanted to go to that other restaurant, but I really wanted to try that new seafood place."

"It's not your fault, Han." Steph drew in a few deep breaths, trying to steady herself. "Is there some water?" Her stomach started to roil as bile crept up her throat. "Oh, no, I think I'm going to be sick."

"Here!" Hannah jumped up and grabbed a bedpan, holding it out for Steph.

But after a few seconds of leaning over the bedpan, the feeling faded.

"I think it must've been the shellfish salad." Steph nodded, holding her protesting stomach. "Especially after I've been on a strict diet to set my system right."

"Steph!" Hannah moaned at her, shaking her head. "What is up with you lately?" Her brow furrowed worriedly. "You've never been into fad diets or trying to get into shape." She ran an eye over her sister. "I don't think you can get into better shape than you already are." She gestured with her hand. "You always do yoga, run, and swim. You're gorgeous and don't need these fad diets."

"It's not a diet," Steph protested. "It's a lifestyle change. I'm forty-three. I have to start changing the way I do things."

"Okay," Hannah held up her hands in surrender. "Just don't push yourself into a skeleton."

"It's not that kind of diet," Steph assured her and looked around the room. "I hate doctors' offices."

"I know," Hannah told her. "But you collapsed, and I wasn't taking any chances."

"Thank you, Han." Steph smiled warmly before glancing impatiently at the door. "Where is the doctor? I have to collect the twins soon."

"Lorry is going to collect them," Hannah told her.

"Oh, no." Steph looked pained. "You told the family I'm at the doctor?"

"No, I told our oldest sister you were at the doctor," Hannah said. "After Lorry called me to find out where you were and when you were getting back to the hotel."

"Of course." Steph shook her head. "Because It's my turn to collect the kids from the horse ranch."

"Not anymore, it's not." Hannah pursed her lips and raised her eyebrows. "I told Lorry you may have food poisoning, so she's gone to fetch them and said you must take the rest of the day off."

"Awesome!" Steph sighed, knowing she would be bombarded with calls from the other four of her sisters, her mother, and her grandmother to find out how she was. "My afternoon isn't going to be easy now, fending off calls from the family finding out how I am."

"Aren't you staying at Scott House pool house while your house is being renovated?" Hannah asked.

"Yes," Steph confirmed.

"Well, then, as soon as you get back to Scott House, you can tell everyone all at once how you are," Hannah pointed out. "And I'll call Ashley and Jess to let them know after the doctor has told us what is up with you."

"Thanks, sis," Steph said as she sighed in relief, suddenly feeling terribly tired.

Hannah's phone rang and she pulled it from her pocket.

"Oh, It's Vince." Hannah pointed at the phone. "I have to go outside the clinic to take this." She looked at Steph questioningly. "Are you going to be okay?"

"Of course." Steph waved her off.

As Hannah left the room to take a phone call, the air in the small examination chamber felt close and confined. The hum of fluorescent lights and the occasional clatter of a distant gurney filled the silence.

Steph sat back with her feet stretched in front of her. Her thoughts drifted through the haze. With Hannah out of the room, she had a moment to absorb her peculiar situation. What could have caused her to faint? Her health had been relatively stable, and she didn't remember feeling ill before the incident.

The door swung open and a doctor entered. He wore a white coat that rustled softly with his movements. His features were kindly, and his eyes held a warmth that put Steph at ease.

"Good afternoon, Ms. Victor," the doctor greeted her, checking her chart. "I'm Dr. Reynolds. Your sister mentioned that you fainted?"

Steph nodded, her voice a mere whisper. "I did, but I don't know why."

Dr. Reynolds proceeded to ask her a series of questions about her health, any recent changes in her life, and her medical history. Steph provided what answers she could, but her memory was muddled.

After some discussion, the nurse called Dr. Reynolds away to get Steph's test results. As he left the room, Steph couldn't shake the lingering unease. Why had her body betrayed her like this?

The minutes dragged on, and Steph felt a growing sense of isolation. The silence in the room pressed in on her, and she closed her eyes, trying to find solace in the darkness behind her lids.

When Dr. Reynolds returned, he carried a folder in his hand. The expression on his face was more serious than before, a hint of concern in his eyes.

"Ms. Victor, I have the results of your tests," he began gently. "Your vitals seem stable, and we couldn't find any immediate health concerns."

Steph's brow furrowed. "So, why did I faint?"

Dr. Reynolds paused for a moment as if choosing his words carefully. "During the tests, we discovered something else."

Steph's heart skipped a beat. "What do you mean?"

The doctor's expression softened into a kind smile. "Ms. Victor, you're eight weeks pregnant."

The word hung in the air, and the room suddenly charged with a mixture of shock and disbelief. Steph's mind raced. She was pregnant? The news felt like a thunderbolt, an unexpected revelation that turned her world upside down.

Eight weeks pregnant. Steph couldn't believe it. The realization struck her like a sudden storm. Then, a memory flickered through the haze of her thoughts. The Bahamas trip that Max had surprised her with nine weeks ago. The romance of that vacation, the shimmering waters, and starlit nights, the tender moments between her and Max. Could this be the result of that trip?

Steph's hands trembled as she placed them on her abdomen as if trying to comprehend the life growing within her. A mixture of emotions swirled within her—surprise, fear, and a hint of something else she couldn't quite define.

As Steph waited in the reception area for Hannah to return from her long telephone conversation, anxiety gnawed at her. Her mind raced and her emotions were in turmoil. She wasn't ready to tell her family about this yet. She had her own relationship woes, and Steph wasn't sure if this was the right moment to share her own unexpected news.

When Hannah returned, her red hair flowing like a river of fire, she looked at Steph with expectant eyes. "What did the doctor say?"

Steph's voice wavered. "I need some supplements for the dizziness, but it's nothing serious. I'm just a little dehydrated, and you were right—it's probably that crazy diet. I also have an appointment for a checkup soon. I have to take it easy for the rest of the day."

Hannah nodded, concern evident in her violet eyes. "Good to hear. We should get you back home, then."

Steph hesitated for a moment, her mind a battlefield of emotions. Then, she managed a faint smile and averted her gaze. "Hannah, when we get to Scott House, would you please let everyone know? I want to go straight to bed. I think I need a little time to myself today."

Hannah regarded her sister with understanding. "Of course, Steph. You know where to find me if you need anything."

As they left the clinic, Steph's mind raced with thoughts of the tiny life growing inside her. Her world had shifted dramatically in a matter of hours, and she needed time to process this newfound reality on her own. Her family's reactions could wait. For now, she wanted to come to terms with this life-changing news privately.

Steph leaned back in the passenger seat of Hannah's car as the familiar sights of Marco Island passed by. The sunny streets, lined with palm trees, felt different now. The world had shifted, taking on a new dimension she couldn't quite grasp.

As they pulled up to Scott House, Steph felt a mixture of relief and trepidation. Her family's support was unwavering, and she knew she could rely on them if needed during this unexpected journey. Only Steph wasn't too sure what that journey would be right now.

She turned to Hannah and managed a weak smile. "Thank you for everything today, Han. I'll see you soon."

Hannah reached out and squeezed her sister's hand. "Take your time, Steph. I'll let everyone know."

With a heavy heart, Steph stepped out of the car, took a deep breath, and began the short walk to the pool house. The lush garden surrounding her was in full bloom, a riot of colors and fragrances. For a moment, the beauty of her family's home provided a soothing backdrop to the tumult of emotions inside her.

Entering the pool house, the memories of the past flooded her mind. The spacious living room was adorned with photos, capturing moments of laughter, love, and family gatherings. Steph's gaze settled on one particular picture, a snapshot of her twin sons, Jack and Liam, from a few years ago. They were inseparable, their faces radiating pure mischief and joy. She sighed, thinking about how they'd react to the news of a new sibling.

But as her fingers brushed the photograph's surface, her mind wandered back to a time of profound struggle that had cast a long shadow over her life.

Fourteen years ago, her life had nearly been shattered during her first pregnancy. What should have been a time of excitement and anticipation turned into a harrowing ordeal. She remembered the terror, the uncertainty, and the relentless pain.

Steph was in her twenties, blissfully in love with Max, and full of dreams. The anticipation of becoming parents had filled their days with joy. But then came the complications. The medical terms had blurred into a dizzying maze of confusion, and the doctors' faces had lost their reassuring smiles.

Her high-risk pregnancy had escalated into a nightmare. Max, a firefighter and paramedic at the time, was her pillar of support through the turbulent months. But even his unwavering strength had faltered in the face of a situation neither of them was prepared for.

She remembered the day they rushed to the hospital. The emergency room was a blur of frantic doctors and nurses. The twins were coming prematurely, and the risks loomed large.

Steph had been on the verge of losing both her children, the very thought, a devastating weight on her heart. The memory of their fragile, newborn forms filled with tubes and wires was etched deep within her soul.

The twins' survival was a miracle, but the experience had taken a toll on Steph. It wasn't just the twins' lives that had been under threat as Steph suffered from postpartum hemorrhage that nearly took her life. It was not just her body that had been scarred; it was her spirit. While she'd heard all the beautiful stories of pregnancy and childbirth from family and friends, all Steph could remember was the terror and pain. And now, faced with the prospect of another high-risk pregnancy, those old fears resurfaced like relentless ghosts from the past.

Steph made her way to the bedroom, her heart heavy with the burden of these memories. She lay on the bed, the room bathed in soft, golden light from the large window overlooking the garden. Her thoughts drifted back to the present, to the tiny life growing inside her, and she wrestled with the uncertainty of her marriage.

Max, once her rock, had been slowly drifting away since the incident that forced his early retirement as a firefighter. Their relationship had become fragile, teetering on the precipice of something unknown. Steph had long felt the strain. Still, she'd been reluctant to address it, fearing it might shatter the illusion of their picture-perfect family life.

Now, with the weight of her unexpected pregnancy adding to the turmoil, she was faced with choices she wasn't sure she'd ever be prepared to make. The uncertainty was unbearable, and she drifted into a restless sleep, hoping that her dreams might offer some clarity or respite from the decisions looming on the horizon. The journey ahead would be fraught with challenges and uncertainty.

CHAPTER 2

Max was deeply entrenched in the bustling world of the Marco Island Marine Center, a sanctuary for him after spending time at the pool house of Scott House. The mysteries of marine life and the rhythmic waves of the ocean brought him solace, but today, tranquility gave way to turbulence as a phone call disrupted his peace.

Max's heart raced as he listened to the voice on the other end of the phone, mirroring the frantic concern in the caller's voice as they explained Steph's sudden collapse. It was an inconceivable scenario for Max, who thought of Steph as someone who never fell ill.

Anxiety gnawed at him, intensified by the vivid memory of his father receiving a similar call a few years ago, just hours before his mother's fatal aneurysm. Hannah's reassurances about Steph's less dire condition, attributed to her recent diet, offered only a modicum of solace.

As he packed up his belongings, Max wrestled with his insecurities, which had deepened like scars after the life-threatening fire that had not only marred his body but had also created a chasm between him and Steph. Memories of the first six arduous months post-accident haunted him when his injuries transformed him into someone he barely recognized. Steph's initial hesitance to draw close to him was understandable, but as he embarked on the path of recovery, she continued to distance herself.

The past two years had been a constant state of trepidation for Max, wary of Steph leaving him. Part of the man he had once been had been devoured by the flames that had ended his career. His body had been seared with scars on his back, leg, and side.

His deepest was that the parts of him that had been reduced to ash by that unforgiving fire were the very elements that bound their hearts together as soulmates. He had changed and was still learning to grapple with this new Max. But his gravest apprehension was that Steph might never embrace, or be able to love, the man he had become.

Max smiled as he remembered their trip to the Bahamas nine weeks ago. He had surprised Steph with the vacation, a desperate endeavor to rekindle their bond. Max knew Steph still loved him, and she remained a devoted wife and mother. But lately, he watched as Steph engaged in dieting, running, and yoga. She had even changed her stunning long hair into a stylish bob that brushed her shoulders.

He couldn't help but feel she was changing. Max pushed away that nagging thought, clenching his jaw. He was perhaps paranoid; Steph had always taken good care of herself, and now that she was over forty, she might believe she needed to exert more effort.

However, the insidious notion that she might be gearing up to leave him nagged persistently. They had enjoyed a blissful week together in the Bahamas. Almost every hour was filled with fun, adventure, and laughter, while their nights had been woven with romance and enchanting moments.

Max sighed and fished out his car keys from the desk drawer. The Bahamas now felt like nothing more than a distant dream, fading as swiftly as it had come to life. He moved to leave his office when a knock at the door sounded, and Kendal James stepped inside, her vibrant enthusiasm clashing with the growing anxiety that gripped him.

"Max, I've got a whole stack of paperwork that needs your signature," Kendal said, her ever-present energy radiating as she plonked a pile of documents on his desk.

Max ran a hand through his hair, his gaze darting back to his phone. "Kendal, I have an emergency at home. Can you please talk to Clyde about this? He can help you with the paperwork."

Kendal leaned in, her voice lowering as she took a step closer. "Max, I've also got some news about the turtles coming in. I think you'd want to hear it from me."

Despite the urgency of the situation at home, Max paused, captivated by Kendal's words. She had a way of making even the mundane aspects of marine biology sound like thrilling adventures. However, his concern for Steph was paramount.

Max made a hasty decision. "I need to go, Kendal. Clyde will help you with everything. We can talk about the turtles later."

Kendal's lips curved into a polite smile as Max hastily exited his office. Outside, Clyde, his ever-observant assistant manager, arched an eyebrow, clearly amused by the situation. "Kendal seems to have quite a soft spot for you, doesn't she?"

In a rush and still weighed down by his concerns, Max waved off the comment with a casual shrug. "You know Kendal, Clyde. She's incredibly passionate about marine life and a valuable team member."

Yet, as he hastened away from the marine center, he couldn't quite shake the lingering thought that maybe Clyde had a point. There had been moments when Kendal's friendliness had felt just a bit too warm, her smiles more lingering. But Max had dismissed those instances as nothing more than her friendly nature. As he pulled out of the center's parking lot, his worries about Steph took precedence, and Kendal's presence soon faded into the background.

When Max arrived at Scott House, he skillfully navigated through the manicured lawns, avoiding any encounters with Steph's family members. He had great affection for the Scott family, but today, he was too worried about Steph for pleasantries.

As he reached the pool house, his heart hung heavy as he thought about the setback the rainstorm that had unexpectedly hit Marco Island had caused the renovations of their own home. While Max was grateful to have a place to stay while their house was being renovated, it wasn't supposed to be for as long as it had been. He longed for the privacy of their own home.

Granted, it was a few feet away from Scott House, but it was still their private haven, separated from Scott House by the Scotts Hotel. Max stepped into the house, throwing his keys on the side table and plopping his briefcase against it. He quietly made his way toward their bedroom.

The gentle Florida breeze rustled the curtains, bringing in the scent of nearby flowers and the faint sound of waves rolling onto the shore.

Max looked around the room, his gaze shifting from the softly swaying curtains to the bed where Steph slept.

Their temporary living situation, necessitated by the unforeseen delays in their home's reconstruction, had stretched on longer than expected. As the days turned into weeks and then months, it felt as if the chasm between them had grown with each passing moment.

The unfinished renovations in their own house, tools, and materials stacked in disarray mirrored the emotional disruption between them. What was supposed to be a minor inconvenience had become a representation of the growing disconnect they both felt.

Max yearned for a return to the intimacy they once shared, for the restoration of the love that had defined their relationship for years. He wished to rebuild the bridge that now seemed so fragile, to rediscover the passion that had once held them together.

Silently, he moved towards the bed, careful not to disturb the tranquility of the room. Steph lay there, a vision of serenity in her slumber. Her vulnerability, even in sleep, pulled at Max's heartstrings.

Memories of their trip to the Bahamas just nine weeks ago surged back into his thoughts. The shared laughter, the thrill of adventure, the depth of their love—those moments felt like a distant dream now. The time spent on the beach, diving into crystalline waters, and the warmth of their embraces served as a poignant reminder of what they had once been and what they could be again.

Max's heart ached for the closeness they had shared, for the passionate connection that had once defined their love. He yearned to hold Steph, to let go of his fears and insecurities, and to rediscover the genuine bond they had cherished.

However, he knew that the issues between them were not just about physical scars or the changes in Steph's appearance. Emotional barriers had grown, silencing communication and pushing them further apart. It was time to confront these issues, to tear down these invisible walls that separated them.

Max reached out and tenderly brushed a strand of hair from Steph's face. Deep in his heart, he hoped they could rekindle the love that had been their foundation to reignite the warmth that had sustained them for so long. Max leaned down and gently kissed Steph's brow.

"I love you, Steph," Max whispered.

He straightened and was tiptoeing from the room when Steph's sleepy voice stopped.

"Max?"

Max turned to see her stretching and stifling a yawn. She reminded him of a kitten stretching in a sunny spot.

"Hey!" Max walked back to her.

"What's the time?" Steph said, her eyes springing wide open, and she sat up.

"Don't get up," Max told her. "I came home early after Hannah called to let me know you'd fainted and ended up at the doctor."

"Oh!" Steph cricked her neck. "You didn't have to break your day for that," she told him. "It was nothing." She gave him a tight smile. "I know how busy it is at the center."

"Of course I'm going to break the day when I get told you landed at the doctor." Max frowned.

"I promise you, it's nothing serious," Steph told him, and he knew she understood why he would've reacted like he did at being told she'd passed out. "The boys!"

"Hannah told me that Lorry went to pick them up." Max wanted to pull her into his arms and crush her lips with his, but he stopped himself. She looked so beautiful. "How about we order in tonight? I know the boys would love it."

"That sounds like a great idea," Steph told him. "And we need to get a nice sticky dessert."

Max's frown deepened as he gave her a curious look. "I thought you were on a metabolism reset diet."

"The doctor told me I had to quit it." Steph stood and straightened the pillows.

"I'm glad," Max told her. "You don't need to change anything about yourself."

"What were you thinking of for take-out?" Steph ignored his compliment as she walked toward the bathroom connected to their bedroom. "Or should we wait to ask the boys?"

"I think we should wait for them," Max suggested. "You know that whatever we order will be wrong."

"Gone are the days when they loved everything we did for them." Steph sighed and shook her head nostalgically.

"I do miss those days." Max laughed. "I must admit that I envy Nicky having a new baby, as it's been nice to have a baby in the family again."

"Yes!" Steph's abrupt answer made his frown deepen. "She didn't have to endure the danger of giving birth."

Before he could say more, she stepped into the bathroom and shut the door, leaving Max staring after her, wondering what that was all about. A sound from the hallway told him the twins were home and unhappy with each other as they were bickering.

"Hey, guys!" Max stepped into the hallway.

His twin fourteen-year-old sons, Liam and Jack, instantly stopped arguing and greeted their father.

"Hey, Dad," they said in unison.

"You're home early," Liam commented, and his eyes widened. "Is Mom okay?"

"She's fine," Max assured them. "But let's not stress her out, okay?" His brows lifted. "And that means no arguing or roughhousing inside."

"Sure," Liam said alongside Jack, "Of course, Dad."

"We've decided to get takeout for dinner tonight," Max told them. "What do you two feel like?"

"Pizza!" Liam and Jack said together.

"I knew you were going to say that." Max rolled his eyes. "Why don't you try something new, like Chinese or burgers?"

"We like pizza," Jack answered.

"We don't like noodles. They look like earthworms." Liam shuddered. Like his mother, he didn't like worms. They creeped him out.

"I don't like how oily or sloppy they are." Jack tried not to gag. "And we already had a burger today."

"Maybe we shouldn't have takeout if you've already had some today," Max raised an eyebrow teasingly.

"Aw, come on, Dad," they groaned in unison.

"If it's any consolation, we've been active the entire day, and I'm sure we burned the burger off hours ago," Jack, the brainiac, pointed out.

"Yeah, and I'm starved." Liam rubbed his stomach, his head swiveling toward the kitchen. "I think I need a snack, or I'm not going to make it to dinner."

"I could do with one, too," Jack said.

"Have something semi-healthy," Max ordered.

"Sure, Dad," Jack called over his shoulder as he and Liam dumped their bags in the door of their rooms and took off toward the kitchen.

Steph stepped out of their bedroom and Max turned toward her.

"Did I hear my ba..." Steph's face seemed to pale, and she swallowed. "My sons?"

Max's brow crinkled, and his head tilted as he looked at Steph, wondering what was going on with her. While she tended to avoid contact with him as much as possible or moved out of his way if they bumped into each other, she wasn't usually jumpy—and now she was jumpy. Max pushed his thoughts to the back of his mind as he followed her down the hallway to the kitchen, where the twins were caught with a jar of peanut butter.

"Hey, you two." Steph's smile warmed and lit up her eyes.

She stepped into the kitchen, skillfully caught the jar of peanut butter, and greeted the twins with hugs and kisses. Max had never been envious of the attention Steph gave them until that minute when he'd have given anything for her to look and greet him like that again.

"Dad says we're getting takeout for dinner," Liam said, stepping out of her embrace and taking the peanut butter.

"PBJ isn't healthy," Max pointed out, standing on the opposite side of the kitchen counter, watching the action.

"Peanut butter isn't bad for you," Jack told him. "And jam gives us energy."

"You two definitely don't need more energy." Steph laughed at their sons. "If I had a bit of the energy you two had, I'd get three times as much done in a day."

Max watched the three of them, his heart swelling as it always did at the sight. Liam and Jack were tall for their age. Max was six-three, and by the look of them, his sons would be just as tall. They already stood nearly a head taller than Steph's five-foot-six frame and loved pointing it out to her.

While they may have his height, they shared their mother's auburn hair and blue eyes. Max's smile broadened. He knew he was being biased, but he had a good-looking family, and they made him burst with pride. Steph was the best mother, and the twins adored her. Max and Steph had ensured they had a good relationship with their boys. Max did his best never to miss a game, function, or important date. With him working at the Marine Center, it was a lot more possible now than when he was with the fire department.

"How was horseback riding?" Steph asked the boys as she took over making their sandwiches.

"I rode Midnight," Jack told her. "He's the best horse."

"I rode Tomboy," Liam told her. "Do you think Aunt Nicky would let me ride Storm Chaser?"

Steph snorted. "In your dreams, maybe." She cut his sandwich and handed the plate it was on to him. "She won't even let me ride him."

"Grandad would've let us," Jack's voice lowered, and his eyes shadowed as he mentioned their late grandfather.

"Yeah, he let us ride him a few times after he got Storm Chaser." Liam's voice held a wisp of nostalgia. He wasn't as emotional as his twin brother. "I'd like to ride him again now that I'm older."

"You'll have to charm your aunt into it," Steph advised him, finishing Jack's sandwich.

"That shouldn't be too hard, then." Max sighed and shook his head. "Your aunt spoils the life out of the two of you."

"That was before Riley came along," Liam told them, and his eyes lit with realization. "Maybe she'll need me to ride him now she's so busy with Riley, the bookstore, Mike, and Jade."

"I wouldn't be too sure of that." Steph cleaned up. "Storm Chaser is her other baby."

"I'm going to ask when she takes us riding again," Liam informed them and took a bite of his sandwich. "Great PBJ, Mom."

He kissed her cheek, grabbed water from the refrigerator, and left the kitchen. His brother followed suit, and the two of them went to sit outside near the pool.

"So, I'm guessing we're getting pizza?" Steph finished putting the snack stuff away and wiped her hands on a dishtowel.

"We can get something else if you don't feel like pizza," Max suggested.

"Actually, I feel like pizza," Steph, who didn't enjoy pizza, surprised him by saying.

"Oh!" Max's eyes widened, and his brows shot up. "Sure. Pizza it is, then."

"I'll order if you can fetch it?" Steph asked him, going through the drawer where all the takeout menus were kept to find the pizza menu. "Ah, this place has that sticky-toffee dessert I love."

"I'll find out what Liam and Jack want for dessert," Max offered and walked out to the pool.

"The waves should be good just before sundown," Liam was telling Jack. "Do you want to go surfing before dinner?"

"Yeah, that sounds like a plan." Jack downed the water.

They turned to look at Max as he walked toward them.

"Want to come for a surf with us, Dad?" Liam asked him.

"I have to go get the food," Max told them, disappointed he couldn't join them. He loved surfing with his sons. "Mom wants to know what you want for dessert?"

"Where are we ordering from?" Jack looked at him.

Max told them, and they both answered that they wanted the same as their mother, only with ice cream.

"Dad!" Jack stopped Max from going back inside.

Max turned to look at his son, who beckoned for him to come closer.

"What happened with Mom?" Jack's voice was low as he asked, his eyes flicking toward the door.

"She fainted," Max told them honestly.

"Mom fainted?" Liam looked at him in disbelief. "I didn't believe Aunt Hannah when she told us that." His brow creased in a worried frown. "Mom *never* faints."

"Nor is she ever sick," Jack pointed out, his eyes also filled with concern.

"She's okay," Max assured them with a warm smile. "It was the silly diet she's been on."

"Mom doesn't need to diet." Jack pulled a face. "She's gorgeous."

"Yeah, all our friends are always saying what a hot mom we have," Liam bragged, making Max laugh.

"Liam!" Jack hissed at him. "Have some freakin' respect, man."

"What?" Liam scowled at his brother. "I'm proud of Mom."

"So am I," Jack told him. "But I don't have to speak about her like she's a cheerleader."

"Hey, you two." Max flashed them a warning look, knowing they were bordering on an argument. "What did I say about not stressing Mom out?"

"Sorry," they both grumbled.

"I'm glad Mom's okay," Jack told him.

"Me too," Liam added. "We were worried about her when Aunt Lorry fetched us and told us Mom was ill."

"She's fine," Max assured them again. "But I'll keep an eye on her, and when I'm not here, I hope the two of you will as well."

"Of course," they answered.

Max smiled, and as he walked back into the house, Steph rushed by him. Her face was gray as she held her stomach, heading for their bedroom. Fear gripped him as he followed her to the bedroom, closing the door behind him as he saw she'd rushed into the bathroom. A few seconds later, his worry grew as he heard her being violently ill.

CHAPTER 3

The morning air was crisp, tinged with the invigorating scent of the sea. Shrouded in the embrace of solitude, Steph slipped out of the pool house before Max and the twins stirred from their slumber. With gentle fingers, she affixed a note to the front of the polished, gleaming refrigerator. The kitchen, still bathed in the soft, early light of dawn, held the promise of the day's first cup of coffee and the quiet anticipation of breakfast conversations.

The note, a silent message to her family, announced her intention to meet with the hotel contractor, a half-truth to make her feel better about avoiding Max. Steph had wanted to play a more active role in the hotel's renovation. Steph found herself drawn to the process, reveling in the opportunity to contribute her ideas to watch the changes unfold not just in her home but also next door. So, it wasn't all an excuse to escape a million questions from Max.

Yet, a voice, uninvited but persistent, echoed in the depths of her thoughts, casting shadows of doubt. It taunted her, calling her a coward for avoiding the complexities of her life. An internal debate raged within her, and in a moment of exasperation, Steph couldn't help but mutter a retort.

"Okay, so I'm not being honest. But I need to sort my head out," was her whispered rebuke to her inner critic! "This is hard for me."

With determined steps, Steph moved away from the kitchen and toward her destination—the hotel that stood just a stone's throw away from Scott House. The journey was short, but the scenery along the way was far from ordinary.

The cobblestone path wound through well-tended gardens, where the riot of colors painted by various blossoms was a feast for the eyes. Tropical blooms intermingled with native flora, and the vivid hues danced harmoniously with the light morning breeze. Their fragrances, a symphony of nature, teased Steph's senses and lent an air of tranquility to her solitude.

As she approached the hotel, its stately facade came into view. The grand structure was an embodiment of timeless elegance, its architecture marrying past traditions with modern comforts. The renovation project was in full swing. Workers, dressed in paint-splattered overalls and construction helmets, moved with purpose. The rhythmic sounds of hammers and drills intermingled with laughter and voices, filled the air.

The renovation breathed new life into the old, revealing glimpses of the hotel's grandeur. Steph watched with a satisfied smile, her heart swelling with the promise of rejuvenation. She had always admired the hotel, a silent witness to the passage of time on Marco Island, and now, she was determined to be part of its transformation. And Steph needed to hide from the shock of her news and let it settle before she made any decisions.

As she stepped into the grand foyer, sunlight streamed through the windows, casting intricate patterns on the tiled floor. The lobby, filled with a sense of history, was a place where memories and dreams intertwined. Amidst the workers and scattered tools, the grandeur of the past was being coaxed back to life.

Steph stood in the middle of the noise, determined to be part of this transformation. The challenges in her life were not dissimilar to the renovations, and like the hotel, she too could undergo a renewal if she dared to confront her fears.

"Steph?" Lorry's eyes widened when she saw her sister, startling Steph. "This is a bit early for you, isn't it?"

"No," Steph denied, shaking her head. "I've come in earlier a lot of times."

"Yes, but that wasn't the day after you collapsed and ended up in the doctor's office," Lorry reminded her.

"I'm fine," Steph assured her.

"Ah!" Lorry nodded knowingly. "You escaped early to avoid being detained by your husband and sons."

"No!" Steph frowned and shook her head. "I wanted to be here when the architect got here."

"Don't remind me *he's* coming here today," Lorry huffed. "The man is insufferable."

"No, he's not." Steph gave her older sister a curious look. "I think he's sweet." She grinned as she ducked into her office to put her purse away before resurfacing. "Not to mention incredibly handsome."

"Does your husband know you come out early to ogle other men?" Lorry teased. "Especially when you landed not only one of the most handsome but nicest men in the world."

Steph swallowed and took a mental breath to steady her nerves. While she couldn't deny what Lorry had said was true, Steph wasn't quite sure she still had him. She forced a smile and quickly moved the subject away from her relationship with Max.

"Why are you fighting Mom and the architect on the expansion plan?" Steph asked Lorry. "You wanted to expand."

"I wanted to renovate and refresh the hotel," Lorry pointed out. "I didn't want to change the structure."

"You won't be changing the structure," a deep voice had them both turning to see Tom Barnes, the architect, dressed in jeans and a cotton shirt, walking toward them. "You'll be adding to it."

"Same thing," Lorry's shoulders instantly stiffened, and her chin raised. She glanced at her wristwatch before looking at Steph. "I'm glad you're early. If you want to be more involved with the hotel renovations, could you deal with this today?"

"Sure." Steph's frown deepened at her sister's icy attitude toward Tom. She turned toward him. "Hi, Tom. I apologize for my sister's rudeness." She shook her head. "I'm not sure what bee is in her bonnet today. At a guess, I'd say it was my niece."

"Hi, Steph," Tom greeted her. His eyes crinkled at the corners as his lips turned into a smile, making him even more handsome. "You don't have to make excuses for Lorry. I know it's me that she doesn't like."

"No." Steph waved his thoughts off. "She's a bit put out that my mother wants to add to the hotels, and my Gran's vote swung it." She smiled. "That's all."

"That's sweet of you to say, Steph." Tom's grin widened. "But your sister took one look at me and decided she didn't like me."

"I think it's men in general that my sister doesn't trust." Steph decided to move the conversation away from her ill-mannered sister. "How are the plans for the extension coming along?"

"That's what I have here." Tom held up the roll of paper he had in his hands.

"Why don't we go to the dining room and grab a coffee—" Steph stopped herself. "Or tea, and you can show me. The tables are bigger there."

"Sure," Tom said, stepping aside for Steph to precede him.

When they got to the dining room, Steph decided it wasn't a good idea as the smell of bacon and eggs hit her, and her stomach started to churn.

"Uh…" Steph tasted the acrid bile rising in her throat. "Will you excuse me for a minute?"

"Not a problem. I'll grab a coffee and a table." Tom gave her a curious look. "Are you okay?"

"I'm fine." Steph nodded before heading for the bathroom, where she locked the door and vomited in the toilet.

When the retching passed, she rinsed her mouth and took a few complimentary mints in the bathroom. Steph quickly opened a few packets and chewed them before meeting Tom.

She spotted him walking to a table with a tray in his hands, and his plans tucked beneath his arm. Steph tried to ignore the aroma hitting her heightened sense of smell in full force. She swallowed and forced herself forward.

"I got you a pot of ginger and lemon balm tea," Tom told her. "I hope that's okay?" He put the tray on the table. "I didn't know if you wanted anything to eat." He gave her a small smile. "I remember when my ex-wife was pregnant, ginger was the only thing that settled her stomach."

Steph nearly choked at his words as she stared at him in shock.

"How did you…" Steph slid into the seat, her brows tightening.

"The minute we stepped into the room and you smelt the breakfast, you turned gray," Tom explained. "Then you bolted to the ladies' room so fast you nearly knocked poor Mrs. Darling down."

"I ran into Mrs. Darling?" Steph's eyes widened in disbelief as her head shot around the room. His eyes settled on the dear old lady who was basically a permanent resident at the hotel. "Oh no."

"Don't worry," Tom told her. "I apologized and told her you had a bit of an upset stomach."

"Thank you," Steph said, pouring some ginger tea into a cup.

"How far along are you?" Tom asked her, stirring sugar into his coffee.

"Eight weeks," Steph couldn't stop the words from slipping past her lips, and she looked at him startled. "I..."

"Don't worry, your secret's safe with me." Tom gave her a reassuring smile.

"How do you know it's a secret?" Steph asked him, taking a sip of the steaming brew.

"Just a hunch." Tom poured cream into his coffee.

"Please don't tell anyone," Steph said with a sigh. "I haven't even told Max."

"Oh!" Tom nodded, sitting back with his coffee in his hand. "I take it this wasn't planned?"

"No!" Steph stressed, and to her dismay, she felt hot tears spring to her eyes. "I'm sorry." She took a napkin and wiped her eyes. "Everything is a little haywire with me at the moment."

"It's understandable," Tom said, his eyes filled with compassion. "I take it that's why you fainted yesterday."

"Oh great!" Steph threw her hand in the air. "Does everyone on the island know about that?"

"Nope." Tom shook his head. "I was with your mother when she got the call."

"Of course, she had to tell you." Steph laughed.

"She was concerned." Tom took a sip of coffee. "Your mother told me you never get sick or pass out."

"It was a shock to me too." Steph put the cup down, then blurted out, "I'm not sure what I'm going to do."

"I don't understand?" Tom looked at her questioningly.

Before she could stop herself, she told Tom about the birth of the twins and why she and Max hadn't tried to have another child. By the time she'd finished telling him, it felt like a great weight had lifted from her shoulders, and Tom had listened to her without the look she usually got from anyone who knew. The look of pity or judgment about the decision she knew she'd be forced to make. Instead, his eyes mirrored her pain, and his words were filled with compassion.

"I'm sorry you have to go through this, Steph." Tom's eyes never left hers. "I'm here if you need to talk or help."

"Thank you, Tom," Steph sniffed and wiped her eyes. "It feels so good telling someone."

"The ears of strangers tend to be more open to listening and their minds free of any preconceived notions someone who knows you might have," Tom told her.

"We're not exactly strangers, though." Steph picked up the tea to try and stomach another sip, as the first one seemed to have settled her stomach a bit.

"True, but we don't know each other that well either." Tom smiled. "How's the tea working?"

"I do feel better," Steph admitted. "Thank you."

"You're welcome." Tom raised his cup. "We don't have to go over the plans if you're not up to it."

"Oh, no." Steph put the cup down. "I want to." She smiled. "It will take my mind off things."

"If you're sure," Tom said. "May I suggest that we don't go over them here?"

"I agree," Steph finished her tea while Tom finished his coffee.

Tom stood and pulled her chair out for her.

"Thanks," Steph stood, and they left the dining room.

"Why don't we go outside, and I'll show you what your mother and I have marked off for the extension?" Tom suggested.

"That would be great." Steph gave him a grateful smile. "Fresh air is just what I need to get the smell of bacon and eggs out of my system."

Steph and Tom walked out the hotel's back door toward the swimming pool. The extensive gardens stretched out before them.

"Your mother wants a few self-catering cottages out here," Tom told her, opening the one set of plans to show her.

"Those are the self-catering cottages?" Steph looked at the plans for the cottages. "They look wonderful."

"There are two of each type, which are bachelor, one, and two bedrooms," Tom showed her. "Then this one will go on the side of the hotel and is the family unit with three bedrooms. But it won't be a single story so that it won't cause privacy problems with your house next door."

"My house is quite a distance from the hotel." Steph looked to where the cottage was going to be built. "So even if it did go up another story, how our house is built means it won't encroach on our privacy."

"Your mother insists they are all single stories." Tom eyed the grounds with a critical eye. "The renovations of your house are finally moving ahead."

"Yes, barring any more freak storms." Steph shook her head and glanced toward her house.

Her heart longed to move back. She loved being with her family, but having her own space was nice. Her kids also missed their home, and she knew Max was starting to get restless. Steph bit her lip in contemplation of her and Max's future. If they even had a future. A twinge zinged through her heart as she thought of the baby growing inside her. She didn't want Max to feel obligated to stay with her now that she was pregnant.

Steph gave herself a mental shake as panic started creeping up on her, and her heart started to pound while breathing became difficult.

"Steph!" Tom's words sliced through her thoughts. He shoved the plans beneath his arm and reached toward her. "Breathe." His strong hands clasped around her upper arms, and he looked at her. "You're having a panic attack." His voice was gentle. "Take a breath in." He sucked in a deep breath, and Steph followed his lead. "Now, slowly let it out."

They did that a few times before the dizziness from her hyperventilating passed, and she could breathe again.

"Here, sit." Tom gently pulled her into a sitting position alongside him on the grass. "Take a few minutes."

Steph crossed her legs, closed her eyes, and cleared her mind of all thoughts. After a few minutes, the world righted itself again, and she felt more relaxed. Steph slowly opened her eyes, meeting Tom's concerned ones.

"How are you feeling?" Tom's voice was soft.

"Much better," Steph admitted. "Again, I'm sorry." She shook her head. "I seem to be dumping all my woes on you today."

"Hey, it's fine," Tom assured her. "I'm just glad I could help."

"I've just realized that I haven't ever sat on this lawn in all my years." Steph looked around.

"Then you've missed out," Tom teased. "This exact spot has the best view."

"I see that." Steph's smile broadened as she looked toward the ocean. "I know you're joking, but this spot does have a great view of the beach and ocean."

"It does," Tom agreed. "This time of the morning, it's also quite peaceful."

"I think this is the perfect spot for the family unit." Steph looked at Tom. "I think the cottage should have a nice deck so the family renting it can have family meals on it."

"That's a good idea." Tom looked at her, impressed. "I should've thought of that."

"I can imagine it." Steph used her hands to envision it. "A wooden deck that is partly covered." She turned her head. "It could maybe wrap around too so the occupants could have sun loungers on the side to sunbathe."

"I can picture that." Tom nodded. "It would be awesome with a jacuzzi."

"Ooh, we could also rent it as a luxury cottage." Steph grinned as the ideas started to flow. "I'll speak to my mother about it."

"Really?" Tom asked. "That would be great."

"Even if it's just a small splash pool if we can't get a jacuzzi." Steph rubbed her chin thoughtfully. "The only thing about having anything like a jacuzzi or splash pool is we'd need to childproof it."

"Agreed." Tom nodded and was jotting points down on a small notepad he'd pulled out of the pocket of his jeans. "If you're serious about it, I'll start putting some costs together so you can put them forward to your mother."

"Yes, I am." Steph nodded. "We've been asked for self-catering units with a jacuzzi or splash pool." She looked at the ocean stretching out in front of them. "Not everyone likes to swim in the sea."

"They don't know what they're missing." Tom gazed in the same direction as Steph. "I love the sea."

"Do you surf?" Steph asked him.

"Yes." Tom nodded. "I often surf with your sons."

"Oh!" Steph pulled a face. "They never mentioned that."

"They're fourteen." Tom laughed. "I doubt I'm a priority in their minds."

"True." Steph nodded. "Unless it's something that directly affects their lives or is a video game, I think it gets automatically sent to their mind's trash can. Boys!"

"Don't worry. I can assure you teenage girls are no different." Tom let out a breath. "I have a fifteen-year-old daughter, Rosie."

"Yes, I've met Rosie." Steph smiled at him. "She's a lovely young woman."

"That's because you don't live with her." Tom ran a hand through his hair, and she saw the pride shining in his eyes. "But, yes, she's the best, even though she has her moments."

"My twins are great boys, but they love to argue with each other." Steph shook her head and stared at the sea. "But they are also best friends and have each other's backs."

"Rosie would love more siblings," Tom told her. "I try to warn her that more means less for her."

"Do you have siblings?" Steph asked him.

"No, it's just me." Tom gave her a tight smile. "I did have an older brother, Wayne, but he was killed while on a mission in the military."

"I'm sorry." Steph felt awful for prying.

"It's okay. It happened fifteen years ago." Tom's eyes darkened with emotion. "The worst thing about losing him was that I never got to say goodbye." He looked down and drew in a sharp breath. "We were also not on speaking terms at the time."

"Oh, no." Steph didn't know what to say. "My grandmother always says that you never walk away from your loved ones angry or on bad terms as you never know what the next second will bring."

"Trust me, that's so true." Tom nodded. "When I was told Wayne was dead—" He shook his head. "I couldn't believe my last words to him had been horrible."

"I'm sure he knew you loved him." Steph gave him a warm smile and gently touched his arm. "When my dad died, everything I wanted to say to him rushed into my head, and I couldn't believe I'd never have the chance to say them to him." She dropped her hands into her lap and sighed. "My gran believes that they stick around for a while in case we have anything we need to say to them."

"Your gran is quite a spooky person." Tom brought the subject to a lighter one.

"She is." Steph nodded. "At our birthday parties growing up, she loved to have a fortune-telling booth, and our friends loved it."

"I've been told by many people on the island that they go to her for regular readings," Tom said. "They swear by her."

Steph laughed. "Can I let you into a family secret?"

"Sure," Tom said, nodding.

"My grandmother is a qualified psychiatrist," Steph spilled the beans on her grandmother. "While much of what she says seems to come true, my sister Hannah reckons it's just Gran being able to read people so well."

"Oh!" Tom pretended to look disappointed. "Does that mean I won't win the lottery this week?" he teased.

"I guess your chances are as good as anyone's." Steph laughed. Her eyes widened when she noticed the time. "Oh, shoot. I have a doctor's appointment in twenty minutes."

"I take that as our cue to leave." Tom shot to his feet and helped Steph to hers.

As Tom pulled Steph up, she tripped, and Tom's arms shot around her to steady her. As they heard footsteps approaching, they turned, and Steph froze.

CHAPTER 4

Max had showered and was ready for work as he walked into the kitchen expecting to find Steph there, making sure there was breakfast for their sons. Their teenage boys ate like horses. When he stepped into the living room, which ran into the open-plan kitchen, he was surprised to find that she wasn't there.

Max frowned, and worry spurted through him until the smell of freshly brewed coffee drifted toward him, and he wandered into the kitchen. He was getting the milk from the refrigerator when he spotted the note taped to the refrigerator door in Steph's neat handwriting. It read, "I had to get to work early this morning."

Squinting at the note, Max couldn't help but feel a little left out. Steph didn't usually go to work so early, and since yesterday, he'd had this nagging feeling she'd been keeping something from him. While they may have been drifting apart emotionally, Max still knew Steph well, and he could tell when she was hiding something. Her mood, jumpiness, and eye contact avoidance every now and then pointed to it.

Running his hand through his hair, he sighed. Max had forgotten to tell Steph he needed her car today as his SUV was due for a service, and the car company was picking it up today. Max looked at his wristwatch, pursing his lips as he calculated the time. Max had no option. He would have to go to the hotel to let her know in case Steph needed her car. Then she'd have to drop him at work.

He stopped for a second and raised an eyebrow. That would be a great idea, and he could surprise Steph and take her for dinner on their way home. Max knew they needed to talk and sort things out between them. Since they'd got from the Bahamas, things had slid back into the pattern that had been forming since the accident, and they seemed to be becoming a landslide. Max knew he didn't want to lose Steph.

Dinner it was! Max smiled as he went to wake up his surly teenagers, who hated being woken up.

"Hey guys!" Max knocked on Liam's and then Jack's bedroom doors before pushing them open. "Wake up."

"Aw, come on, Dad," Liam grumbled, pulling a pillow over his head. "It's summer vacation. Please let me sleep in."

"I'm with Liam!" Jack called, turning onto his side and fixing his pillow with his back to his father.

"Okay." Max laughed. "But then you're on your own for breakfast."

"We're fourteen, Dad," Jack reminded him. "We can get our own food now."

"Good to know," Max told him. "If I get you takeout again tonight, will you be okay on your own for a couple of hours tonight?"

"Why?" Jack spun around to look at his father.

"I'm thinking of taking your mother out for a surprise dinner," Max informed them.

"I'm sure we'll survive." Jack grinned at Max. "You and Mom need a night out."

"Yeah, we'll go to Gran if we need anything." Liam yawned and started drifting asleep. "See ya, Dad."

"Okay, be good today and careful," Max told them, leaving them to sleep.

Max strolled out of the pool house, eyeing the early-morning sun. His destination was Scotts Hotel, just a short walk away. As he approached the hotel, his mind began to spin a bit faster. Thoughts of what Steph was keeping from him whirled through his mind. Max was so lost in them that he didn't notice the beauty of the day awakening around him or the fresh morning air that skipped along the shore. He was so preoccupied with his thoughts that he nearly knocked Lorry over when he stepped into the cool entry hall of the hotel.

"Max!" Lorry stepped out of his way just in time.

Max's head shot up, and his eyes widened. "Oh, sorry!" He stopped and gave her a tight smile. "Hi, Lorry. I was deep in thought."

"I saw that," Lorry told him. "As you nearly plowed me over." She smiled. "What's the hurry?"

"I'm looking for Steph," Max told her. "She left so early this morning I forgot to let her know that I need a ride to work today as my car is going for a service."

"Steph is dealing with the architect that our mother has doing the expansion." Lorry's shoulders stiffened as she mentioned the project.

"I see you're still opposed to the expansion," Max observed.

"My father wanted us to renovate and refresh the hotel," Lorry's voice turned frosty. "Not turn it into a holiday camp."

"Lorry, a few self-catering or catered cottages don't make the hotel a campsite." Max tried not to smile at the look she shot him. "Sorry, I don't mean to be rude, but I have to find Steph, or I'm going to be late for a meeting."

"Oh, sure," Lorry said, turning toward the hotel's back entrance that led to the pool. "They went out the back so the architect could show her the plans and where they would be built."

"Tom Barnes is the architect's name," Max pointed out, hiding another smile as her eyes flashed icily at him.

"I know that," Lorry said, raising her chin.

Max smiled as Lorry spun on her heel and strolled through the doors, past the pool, and when they didn't see Steph and Tom at the back, they headed for the side of the hotel. The side that Max's and Steph's house was on. He sighed as his heart longed again for the privacy and comfort of his home.

Before they turned the corner, infectious, carefree laughter echoed from behind it. Max knew it was Steph's, and he wondered what had elicited it from her as it was a sound he'd not heard in two years. As Max and Lorry stepped around the corner, the unexpected scene unfolding before him was a cold shock to the system.

Max's heart froze, and a whirlwind of emotions—surprise, confusion, disbelief, and uncertainty made his knees feel weak. As Steph was pulled into Tom's arms, Max felt like an outsider looking in on a moment he shouldn't be witnessing. Max felt the blood drain from his face, and his voice got trapped in his throat when he wanted to call out to Steph. He wanted to demand to know what was happening as his brow creased and his mind tried to make sense of what he was witnessing.

"Steph!" Lorry hissed. Her voice coated in ice. It sent a chill down his spine.

"Max!" Steph breathed, quickly stepping out of Tom's embrace. "What are you doing here?"

Steph walked toward him with Tom in tow as if nothing had happened, while he felt as if someone had staked him in the heart and thrown him in a washing machine filled with too many emotions.

"Your car," Max's voice was gruff as his throat felt dry, and the shock made his system pulse.

"Hi, Max," Tom greeted him with a friendly smile, holding out his hand that Max took automatically.

"Hey," was all Max managed to say before turning toward Steph. "Can we talk?"

"I have to get going," Tom said, looking at his wristwatch before turning to Steph. "I'll draw up the additions, and we can chat as soon as they're done and I've got the costing."

"Thank you, Tom," Steph's face lit up as she smiled at the man.

An emotion Max had never felt before surged through him—jealousy, which pulled a rush of anger with it. He clenched his jaw and tried not to ball his hands into fists at his side, and he struggled to keep his raw emotions in check.

Tom said his goodbyes and left, but Max had to hang on to the words forming on his tongue that was ready to lash out at her while his brain tried to keep calm and instill some rational thought. But his aching heart was bleeding into his wounded soul that was crying out for answers, and where there was once a magical connection between them, there was nothing but silence from Steph.

"Steph, I have to go to a meeting in Naples, and I'm staying over," Lorry informed her. "Would it be possible for Tammy to stay with you tonight, please?"

"Sure," Steph said before Max could say anything.

"Thank you." Lorry breathed a sigh of relief. "She didn't want to stay with Mom because of Nicky's baby." She rolled her eyes. "I miss the younger version of my drama queen teen daughter."

"I can relate at times." Steph laughed. "I miss being able to buy clothes, toys, or anything really for my kids and having them love it." She shook her head. "Now, just because I bought it, it's not cool."

"Don't get me started on that." Lorry held up her hands. "You know how Tammy is when we go shopping."

"I'm sorry to break this up," Max interrupted. "But I need to get to work." He turned to Steph. "Can you take me and pick me up after work tonight?" He forced a smile. "I forgot to tell you last night that my car is going in for a service today."

"Oh, shoot!" Steph hit her head with the palm of her hand. "I actually did remember that, as it's on the calendar." She shook her head. "I have porridge brain today."

"Relax, little sister." Lorry smiled warmly at Steph. "You weren't well yesterday, which is a shock for everyone and you most of all, as you're the super healthy one of us six sisters." She glanced at her wristwatch. "I must go. I still have to stop by the apartment, get Tammy to pack, and get to the pool house."

With Lorry's hurried departure, Max and Steph were left alone in the wake of a tense silence. Max was still shell shocked from witnessing Steph in Tom's embrace, and he wasn't sure how to broach the subject. Uncertainty gripped him as he desperately sought the right words.

Breaking the oppressive quiet, Steph finally spoke. "Max, about the car, you can take it, or I can give you a ride to work. It's your choice."

Max hesitated for a moment. He was torn between a desperate need to talk to her and an equally strong desire to give them some private space away from the prying eyes and ears of their home. "Actually," he began, "I think it might be better if you drop me off at work. It's summer vacation, and I don't want you to be without a car, especially with the kids. I can manage without a car for the day."

Steph nodded, seemingly relieved by his decision. "Okay, but we'd better get going, or you'll be late."

They walked back to the pool house to grab her car keys. As they entered the empty pool house, the sound of the waves crashing against the shore outside seemed to amplify the quiet tension between them. The house was empty, and Max assumed the boys had gone surfing. He knew this was not the moment to address his concerns, as he wanted to shatter the fragile calm between him and Max.

But as Steph walked down the hallway with her car keys in her hand, he could not hold the words in any longer. Max blurted out, "Steph, I need to know, are you having an affair with Tom?"

Steph's face contorted in a mix of astonishment and disbelief. She stared at him, momentarily speechless. "What? Max, where on earth is this coming from? What makes you think that?"

Max's anxiety transformed into frustration, and he couldn't help the edge that crept into his voice. "I saw you in Tom's arms, Steph. You were laughing, and I... I don't know what to think anymore."

Steph's temper flared, and her eyes flashed with irritation. "Are you serious, Max? Are you trying to appease your guilty conscience by accusing me of having an affair?"

Max was taken aback by her counter-accusation, and his confusion was palpable. "What do you mean? I don't understand."

Steph's phone buzzed, lying on the nearby table as if on cue. It was an ill-timed interruption, and Max had to physically restrain himself from grabbing it to see if it was a message from Tom. Instead, he snapped, his frustration getting the best of him, "Is that him, Tom, checking to see if the two of you were busted?"

Furious and clearly upset, Steph threw her car keys at Max, who caught them reflexively.

"You know what, Max? Take my car. I'll borrow my mom's or gran's if I need to go anywhere," she said with a steely determination that he had rarely seen in her. She walked up to him and shoved her phone in his hands. "There you go. Snoop all you want. Heck, pull my phone records, too." Her eyes flashed dangerously. He'd never seen Steph this angry. "You're welcome to go through all my things to see if I have another phone as well. My purse is at the hotel if you'd like to rifle through that."

With that, she pushed past Max and stormed out of the pool house, leaving it filled with tension, unanswered questions, and a heavy sense of betrayal. Max was left holding Steph's phone, contemplating whether to unlock it and see for himself what messages were causing this uproar. But he hesitated, torn between wanting to know the truth, trusting Steph, and respecting her privacy.

Max was ashamed to admit that it took every ounce of control he had to put Steph's phone on the kitchen counter, pick up his briefcase as he headed for the door, and walk to her car. Max's mind was reeling, and he felt as if someone had punched him in the heart, and the world around him seemed to grow dimmer. Like his sunshine had just been eclipsed by their first serious fight in their eighteen years together. Sixteen of which they'd been married for.

As Max drove toward the Marine Center, his mind went over the argument, wondering how it had escalated so quickly and what Steph had meant about him appeasing his own guilty conscience. His brow knit in a tight frown at her words. Max pulled into his parking space at the center and climbed out of the car when Kendal came bounding towards him.

"Hi, Max," Kendal greeted him. "Is that a new car?"

"No, it's my wife's," Max told her. "You're in early today. I thought you were on the afternoon shift."

Max started walking toward the front door with Kendal walking with him.

"I didn't get to talk to you about the turtles yesterday," Kendal told him. "Their recuperation habitat still needs some work to get done in time."

"You know we can't pay you extra time, Kendal," Max warned her as he stepped inside the large entry hall and was greeted by Glenda, his assistant.

"Morning, Max," Glenda smiled at him as she walked toward her office, which was a door away from him. "Would you like a cup of coffee?" she asked over her shoulder.

"Yes, please," Max called after her and was about to follow her when Kendal grabbed his arm, stopping her.

"Wait, Max," Kendal said. "I don't expect to get paid for this time this morning. I want to get the habitat done. I was wondering if you'd help me with it?"

"I'm afraid I don't have time," Max told her. He wasn't in the mood for small talk or over-eager staff members. "Maybe talk to one of the contractors and tell them I gave you permission to get them to help you."

With that, Max stepped around her and walked to his office. When Glenda walked into his office, he'd just sorted out his briefcase and was getting settled in for the day.

"There you go," Glenda placed a steamy mug of coffee on a coaster on his desk. "Don't forget you have a new investor who'll be here in fifteen minutes."

"Mike's hardly that formal, Glenda." Max didn't look up as he shuffled through papers, looking for the contract he'd prepared for Mike.

"Here." Glenda reached over and pulled the document from a pile on the side of his desk. "Is this what you're looking for?"

"Yes, thank you." Max gave her a tight smile. "And thank you for the coffee."

"Are you okay?" Glenda frowned at him worriedly. "You seem on edge and not your usual smiling, calm self."

Max forced another smile onto his protesting face. "Just having a bit of a bad morning."

"Oh dear," Glenda tutted. "Well, take a deep breath, have some coffee, and hopefully, the day will improve." She grinned. "Especially if Mike Sullivan writes the center a big fat check."

"We really need it." Max nodded and picked up the coffee. "When Mike gets here, please show him right in."

"I will," Glenda said and started walking to the door, stopping on the threshold. "How's Steph?"

Max's head shot up at the mention of his wife. His heart slammed into his ribs, wondering if Glenda had somehow guessed they were fighting. When he looked into her eyes, they were brimming with concern, and he realized she was asking about Steph's health.

"She's fine," Max assured Glenda. "Steph's been on this health kick to restart her metabolism after forty and wasn't eating as she should."

"Your wife is the last person that needs that." Glenda smiled. "Steph is gorgeous, and any woman half her age would kill to look like her."

"Thank you, Glenda," Max told her. "I'll pass that on to her."

With that, Glenda left his office, closing the door behind her. Finally left in solitude, Max sank back against the plush office chair, trying to quiet his buzzing mind. His phone rang, distracting him and making his heart jolt, hoping it was Steph. Disappointment coursed through him when he saw it was Wallis Albright, his lifelong best friend.

"Hey, Wallis," Max answered the phone.

"Hi, Max," Wallis's cheery voice floated through the phone. "Are you free tonight?"

"No, I have some family issues to deal with," Max told him. "Why?"

"My wife and kids are out of town, and I was wondering if you wanted to watch the ballgame over at mine tonight?" Wallis invited.

"I'd love to," Max answered honestly. "Let me see what happens when I get home, and I'll call you."

"Great," Wallis said.

"Hey, what do you know about Tom Barnes?" Max couldn't stop himself from asking.

"Not much," Wallis told him. "His father has lived on Marco Island his whole life, but Tom's parents divorced when Tom was a kid, and his mother took him and his brother and moved to Naples."

"That sounds like you know quite a bit about him." Max snorted.

"I know his father," Wallis said. "Tom moved to the island with his daughter after getting divorced some years ago and works for his father's construction company."

"I know that much," Max admitted.

"Why are you asking about Tom?" Wallis asked. "I thought you already had contractors working on the center."

"Oh, no reason," Max clenched his jaw, regretting having asked like a jealous fool. "Tom is doing the plans for the extension of Scotts Hotel."

"Ah, you've decided to stand with Lorry against the expansion," Wallis teased Max.

"Yeah, no!" Max shook his head. "When it comes to being on good sides, I prefer being on my mother-in-law's good side."

"Always the wise choice." Wallis laughed. "Listen, buddy, I have to go, but call me later and let me know if you want to come around for beer, pizza, and baseball later."

"Will do," Max said, hanging up.

The rest of the day flew by with meetings, reports, and building inspections. Max was exhausted and wasn't sure how he'd managed to get through the day with the constant worry about Steph nagging at the back of his mind. He couldn't remember a day when he'd checked his phone nearly every other minute, hoping for a call from Steph.

He was about to leave when Kendal breezed into his office.

"Max, could you have a look at the turtle habitat before you go?" Kendal asked him. "I know how much this project means to you, and I'm hoping I've managed to get it exactly to your specifications."

"Kendal, all the marine life rehabilitation projects are equally important to me," he told her. "And I'm sure you've done a great job on the turtle project, but that's one of Clyde's projects, so you'd have to ask him."

"Clyde's?" Kendal sputtered in disbelief. "But this was supposed to be your special project. That's why I insisted on being part of it and rallied for the sponsorship."

"While I appreciate how much you helped by getting the project funded, you know that Clyde oversees all the rehabilitation projects," Max reminded her again, closing his briefcase, pulling the car keys from his drawer, and heading out with Kendal trailing behind him.

"What projects are you working on, Max?" Kendal persisted.

"I have other work going on at the moment, and I've delegated the research center to be overseen by Clyde," Max informed her, irritated by her refusal to listen. "Will you excuse us, please, Kendal? I have to speak to Glenda before I leave."

Without waiting for her response, Max ducked into Glenda's office, missing the narrowed-eye look Kendal shot his way.

"Glenda, I'm heading home," Max told her, handing her a folder. "Here are all the forms from some great new investors."

Glenda took the folder from him, grinning as she went through it. "It looks like you've had quite the lucrative day."

"It was." Max gave her a tight smile. "I'll see you tomorrow."

Max left the center and headed home, wondering if he should stop and buy some flowers for Steph or if she'd consider going to dinner with him that night. He let out a nervous breath, not knowing what to expect when he arrived home. Before today, Max and Steph seemed to have fallen into a pattern of tiptoeing around each other. At least he knew what to expect with that pattern. What had happened between them this morning had fractured whatever little peace was left between them.

When Max pulled into Scott House's driveway, he noticed that Hannah's car was missing and remembered she was going back to Palm Springs that day. A pang of guilt rushed through him as he hadn't said goodbye. Max made a mental note to message her later and find out if she got home safely as he made his way to the pool house. Max was glad he'd not run into one of the Scott family members as he slipped into the pool house.

Max put his briefcase down where he always did near the door and Steph's keys on the side table. His brow creased as a heavy silence greeted him, and before even looking through the rooms, Max knew there was no one home. Not wanting to read anything into it, he walked into the kitchen and froze when he saw the note taped to the refrigerator door.

Max, the boys, Tammy, and I have decided to take Hannah up on her offer to spend a few days with her in Palm Beach. I'll get the twins to call you when we're there.

Steph

Max's hand shook as he ripped the note from the refrigerator door. He was rereading the note when his phone dinged, and he absently pulled it from his pocket. It was a message from Steph.

After this morning, I think we need some space to get our heads right. We need to talk when I'm back in four days to a week.

Max put his phone on the counter and leaned against it with both hands. Pain shot through his heart straight into his soul as one thought rushed through his mind—Steph was thinking about leaving him.

CHAPTER 5

They had been driving for three hours, and Steph was so glad when they pulled into the driveway of Hannah's Wellington home. She felt queasy and needed a cold glass of water and to stretch her legs.

"Wow!" Liam, Jack, and Tammy chorused as they stepped out of the car and looked at Steph's large modern Spanish-style house.

"I love your new house, Aunt Hannah," Tammy told her.

"I liked your house in Key West," Liam said as Hannah pooped the trunk and the kids pulled their luggage from it.

"I do, too," Hannah admitted.

"This one is very showy," Steph commented, smiling appreciatively as Jack took her suitcase and Liam took Hannah's.

"It's a lot bigger than the one in Key West," Hannah told them, leading the way inside through the double wooden door.

The entrance hall was spacious, with marble tiles that led throughout the house. Five doors led off the hall with a staircase sweeping up the right wall. Ceiling-to-floor windows could be seen through the back three entrances.

"On the left is the television room. To the right is my home office." Hannah talked them through the house. "The door after the office is a cloakroom and bathroom." She pointed to a facing door on the left. "That's the kitchen, breakfast room, and sunroom." She pointed straight ahead. "As you can see, that's the dining room." She pointed to the door on the right. "That's the main living room." She smiled at them. "It leads through to the entertainment area, indoor pool, and to the outdoor kitchen and barbeque area."

"Do you have a sauna and gym?" Liam asked.

"Yes." Hannah nodded. "Through the pool room."

"Cool!" Liam, Jack, and Tammy said in unison.

"On the first floor is my bedroom and three guest bedrooms." Hannah looked at Steph and Tammy. "Steph, you and Tammy can take a room on that floor." She grinned at the twins. "While the two of you get to use the two bedrooms on the second floor."

"Awesome!" Jack said as he, Liam, and Tammy headed for the stairs. "Can we go up?"

"Of course." Hannah indicated toward the stairs and looked at Tammy. "Tammy, let Steph have the room directly next to mine. You can choose any of the others."

"Cool." Tammy nodded, and the three of them disappeared up the stairs.

"Wow!" Steph gave a low whistle as she followed Hannah into the kitchen. "Han, this is amazing."

"I sold my house in Key West for a huge profit," Hannah told her as she filled the coffee machine. "I don't know about you, but I could use a cup of coffee."

"Do you have ginger tea?" Steph asked, putting her purse on the white marbled center block in the spacious kitchen.

"I do," Hannah nodded and frowned at her sister, tilting her head slightly. "Steph, what's going on?"

Steph was walking toward the window to look out over the extensive garden. She stopped and turned to look at Hannah.

"I'm fine," Steph tried to assure her but knew not much got past Hannah.

"No, you're not!" Hannah put the kettle on the stove for Steph's tea. "Something's been off with you for a while now." She pulled mugs from a cupboard. "I know that Max getting injured was hard on the two of you."

"Yes, it was," Steph said absently, staring out over the rolling lawns to the summer house at the end of the garden. "You've got a summer house."

"Yeah, it's empty at the moment," Hannah told her, standing beside Steph. "I'm not sure what to do with it."

"What's going to happen when you and Vincent get married?" Steph looked at her younger sister. Her brow furrowed as she saw a look of uncertainty flash in Hannah's eyes.

"What do you mean?" Hannah asked.

"You only bought this house eighteen months ago when you moved from Key West to Palm Beach," Steph commented. "Will Vincent live with you here?"

"We haven't really spoken about it," Hannah admitted. "But I guess it would be the most logical choice, as he has an apartment along the waterfront in West Palm Beach."

"For an engaged couple, you live quite far apart," Steph said.

"It's not that far." Hannah shrugged. "It's only about sixteen miles, and the driving time is about twenty minutes."

"Where is the hospital that you both work at?" Steph followed Hannah back to the center block when the kettle whistled and sat on the tall, white-backed bar stool.

"In the middle." Hannah switched off the stove and poured boiling water into the cup with the tea bag. She picked up the mug and put it in front of Steph. "It's a fifteen-minute drive for me and ten for him."

Hannah got the honey from a cupboard and put it on the counter. She poured herself a cup of coffee and added some milk before sitting on the opposite side of the counter to Steph.

"Mom!" Liam rushed into the kitchen. "You must see our rooms."

"They're awesome," Tammy said, following her cousin into the kitchen.

"I'm glad you like them," Hannah said with a warm smile. "Do you want something to drink or eat?"

"Yes, please," Liam said. "I'm starved."

"I don't have much," Hannah confessed. "I thought your mom and I could go to the store, but we can order something for now."

They settled on pizza, and Hannah ordered it.

"Where's Jack?" Steph asked Liam.

"He's speaking to Dad," Liam told her. "I said hi and told him we were here safe."

"Good." Steph smiled and looked at Tammy. "Did you call your mom?"

"Yup!" Tammy nodded. "She's happy we're safe and gave me the 'be good' lecture."

"While we wait for the pizza, can we go see the games room?" Liam asked.

"Of course," Hannah told him. "Make yourselves at home. If you want to swim, you'll find towels in the pool room."

"Great!" Tammy said as Liam rushed from the kitchen with Tammy hot on his heels.

"Where do they get all that energy from?" Hannah blew out a breath.

"You have a lot of inside space for them to explore." Steph laughed at the expression on her sister's face. "They'll be exploring the grounds next."

"There's a stable at the back of my property," Hannah told her. "I'll take them horse riding before you leave."

"They'd love that," Steph assured her, pouring honey into her tea and taking a sip.

The warm ginger brew settled her queasy stomach.

"It was nice of Lorry to let you leave on such short notice." Hannah grinned, referencing their oldest sister.

"I think she wanted me out of the way so she could try and stop or at least stall the hotel upgrade project." Steph laughed. "She does *not* like Tom or his father, James."

"Lorry doesn't take to change very well." Hannah pursed her lips and raised her eyebrows. "She's been through so much of it in her life that she tries to control what she can."

"Like being a sergeant major running our family hotel." Steph laughed.

"Exactly!" Hannah gestured with her hand. "That's why she isn't happy about the upgrade for the hotel, as Mom is controlling that project, and she feels sidelined."

"Or she just doesn't like Tom or his father." Steph pulled a face. "If I tell you something, it can go no further than the two of us."

"Oh!" Hannah's face lit up at the thought of sharing a secret. "You know I can keep a secret." She snorted. "It's part of my job—keeping secrets."

"Yes, but this one doesn't come with your usual client-patient confidentiality," Steph pointed out.

"Give me a dollar!" Hannah held out her hand.

"Why?" Steph's brow furrowed, and she looked at her sister curiously.

"Then you've hired me, and I have to keep your secret," Hannah told her.

"I thought that was for lawyers," Steph said skeptically.

"Nope, it applies to me as well," Hannah assured her. "Now give me a dollar."

"I'm paying you to keep the secret now?" Steph grumbled.

She pulled her purse on the end of the counter they were sitting at toward her and dug for her wallet.

"Here." Steph handed Hannah the dollar. "One dollar."

"Thank you." Hannah opened a drawer near her and put the dollar into it. "Now, what's the secret?"

"I caught Mom and James on a date last week." Steph grinned at the look of disbelief on Hannah's face.

"No way!" Hannah's voice was barely audible as her eyes darkened with emotion. "Dad's only been gone for a couple of years."

"Hannah!" Steph couldn't believe out of all the sisters, Hannah would be the one to have such an adverse reaction to the news. "Dad's been gone for *three years,* and Mom has been lonely ever since."

"Are you sure it was a date?" Hannah queried, ignoring Steph's reasoning.

"Yes, Hannah, I'm sure it was a date," Steph confirmed and decided not to tell Hannah why she was sure of that.

"Maybe they were having a business meeting," Hannah suggested.

"Out of all of us, as the psychiatrist, you'd be the one to handle Mom dating much better than the rest of us," Steph told her. "Lorry is really protective over Mom and Gran. I think she suspects something is going on with Mom and James." She shook her head, feeling disappointed in her younger sister. "But Lorry is wary of relationships, and I'd expect how you reacted to the news from her."

"How are you so accepting of Mom dating again?" Hannah's eyes narrowed. "You were the biggest daddy's girl out of all of us."

"Thanks!" Steph's eyes widened, and she knew it was time to wrap this conversation up before they got into a sibling fight. "Just forget I said anything." She slid off the chair and picked up her purse. "I'm going to find my room and have a shower. I'm feeling sticky from the drive."

Steph didn't give Hannah a chance to reply as she headed out the kitchen door and up the stairs to the room Hannah had said was Steph's while she was there. She was happy to see the room she'd walked into was the correct one, spotting her luggage. Steph closed the bedroom door and started to unpack her suitcase. Once she was done, Steph hopped into the shower feeling refreshed and not as queasy when she was finished.

Steph had finished getting dressed and was sitting on the ridiculously comfortable bed, brushing her hair, when her phone pinged. She picked it up and saw it was another message from Max. Steph sighed, knowing she'd better message him back, and her heart felt heavy as she read the text.

Steph, I'm glad you got to Palm Beach safely. Please tell Hannah I'm sorry I missed saying goodbye, but I'm sure I'll see her soon. I miss you and the kids. The house is so quiet without all of you in it.

I think I know when, but I'm just not sure how we managed to get to this place in our relationship. But I do know that whatever it takes, I want to work through it. Take whatever time you need, and I'll be here waiting for you to return.

Love

Max

Steph's eyes welled with tears, and she let them roll down her cheeks as she sat staring at Max's message. Her mind was in a turmoil of confusion, and she felt like she was living a bad dream. Max was her one true love, her best friend, and her soulmate. But since the fire that ended his career, he'd changed so much she no longer recognized him. He was paranoid about his scars to the point where he no longer took his shirt off, even to swim if there were people around.

When they were in the Bahamas nine weeks ago, even when they lay in the sun, Max kept his shirt on. When they went diving, he wore a full wetsuit. When Steph had asked him why he didn't want to catch a tan, he'd told her he didn't want to expose his scars to the sun. But Steph knew it went a lot deeper than that for him. Max's scars were not just skin deep, and he refused to talk to *anyone* about it—not even a therapist. He kept trying to assure everyone who tried to get him to seek help that he was fine.

Steph closed her eyes and lay back against the soft pillows, blowing out a breath. Max didn't know that Steph had found his resignation letter to the fire department. She knew that Max wasn't forced to leave because of his injuries. He'd resigned, stating that he no longer felt he had it in him to do the work. When Max had started at the Marine Center, he had thrown himself into the job, and then Kendal was employed. Max's days at the center seem to get even longer after that, not to mention the weekend conferences that he started going to with Kendal and Clyde.

The one weekend Max had told her Clyde was with him and Kendal, Steph had found out Clyde hadn't gone. According to him, the conference had been canceled. That was the day Steph's eyes had been opened to a possibility that she'd never thought possible—Max was having an affair. When Max returned from his weekend at the supposed function, Steph had asked him about it, and he'd waffled on about a new turtle habitat that some company was sponsoring.

Steph had felt her heart start to crack, and it had slowly been splintering into painful shards ever since. She glanced at the message from Max once again and was about to write back when there was a soft knock on the bedroom door.

"Steph," Hannah called through the door. "Can I come in?"

"Sure," Steph replied, putting her phone on the nightstand as her sister entered the room, closing the door with a soft click behind her.

"I'm sorry," Hannah said, her brow crinkling. "You're right. I should've handled the news about Mom and James better."

"It's okay." Steph sighed and patted the bed beside her for Hannah to join her. "It was a shock for me at first too. I went home after seeing her having a romantic dinner with James and waited up for her in the living room of Scott's house."

"You didn't!" Hannah's eyes widened as she climbed onto the bed beside Steph.

"I did!" Steph laughed at her actions, realizing how silly they'd been. "I heard James and Mom at the front door and peeked through the front window." She shuddered. "To my horror, they were—" Her eyes widened, and she looked apologetically at Hannah.

"They were kissing!" Hannah guessed and sighed, grabbing a pillow to hug.

"Yup!" Steph nodded. "I suddenly felt like a snoop and wondered if this was what I would be like when the twins started dating."

"Yes, but wouldn't their girlfriends' parents be the ones spying?" Hannah pointed out.

"Who says a girl can't walk a guy home?" Steph pointed out. "This is a new world after all."

"True!" Hannah nodded. "But you and Max brought your boys up to be gentlemen."

"That's also true," Steph acknowledged. "After spying on Mom and James, I'm worried I may follow my boys or something when they start dating."

"Nah!" Hannah shook her head, disagreeing with Steph. "You're not like that, and you weren't spying on Mom. You were checking to see if it was her at the door."

"I like that scenario better." Steph smiled.

"What happened when Mom came inside?" Hannah looked at Steph questioningly.

"She was surprised to see me," Steph told her. "I lied and told her I needed to borrow some milk as I wanted to make cocoa, and I heard someone at the front door."

"Wow!" Hannah looked at Steph, impressed. "Miss Morals lying!"

"I felt awful," Steph admitted. "But Mom was cool about it and was acting like a giddy teenager. She was so happy to be able to finally tell one of her daughters." She shook her head. "That's when all my shock and anger at Mom betraying Dad faded." She smiled at Hannah. "I realized that Mom is only in her late sixties, and she is so young and active for her age that, of course, she'd want to date again."

"You are so right," Hannah sighed and squeezed the pillow. "Mom deserves to be happy again. Gran won't be around forever, and we've all moved out and have our own lives."

"James is a terrific man," Steph told her. "He's kind, caring, considerate, and an absolute gentleman." She grinned. "I did some digging on him and his previous marriage."

"You didn't!" Hannah gaped at Steph in amazement. "Who are you, and what have you done with my little Miss Perfect sister?"

"I'm far from perfect, little sister," Steph assured her. "I was obsessed with ensuring that if Mom was dating, she was dating a man that would stand up to Dad."

"You investigated James?" Hannah nodded in understanding. "What did you find?"

"Exactly what I told you about him." Steph bit her lip. "James Barnes is a hard-working man who is well-liked, like Dad was."

"That's good to know," Hannah replied.

Something about her demeanor set off warning bells in Steph's mind.

"You're going to investigate James as well, aren't you?" Steph guessed.

"Maybe I can find something you may have overlooked," Hannah told her. "Next time I go home, I'll be sure to keep a close eye on him."

"Translation—you're going to psychoanalyze the poor man." Steph laughed.

"Like you said, we can't have our mom dating just any man!" Hannah looked at Steph.

"We actually shouldn't be interfering *at all*," Steph advised. "Mom is a grown woman, and we can't tell her what to do or who to date."

"Yes, but we can make sure she's not getting herself into a difficult, or worse yet, dangerous situation," Hannah defended their actions before asking, "Do any of our other sisters know?" Her eyes widened. "Does Gran know?"

"I think Lorry suspects something, but you know Lorry, she'll turn a blind eye until the truth slaps her in the face," Steph answered. "But I don't think any of our other sisters know. Nicky's too caught up with her new family, romance, and bookstore." She raised her eyebrows. "Ashley and Jess haven't been home since Christmas."

"It's just you and me that know." Hannah tilted her head thoughtfully. "I agree that we must keep this a secret for as long as possible." She looked at Steph. "Or at least until Mom decides to tell us."

"I'm sure she will when she's ready," Steph said. "I did tell her I wouldn't say anything."

"Except to me," Hannah teased. "Speaking of relationships—" She caught Steph's eye. "When will you tell me why you suddenly decided to fly the coop and run away to Palm Springs?" She held up her hands. "Not that I'm complaining. I love having you and the kids here. But I can't remember a time when you and Max have been apart."

Steph pursed her lips, contemplating what to tell Hannah. Out of all her sisters, Hannah would be the one that would understand as well as being more qualified to help.

"Please don't tell me you need space from your perfect marriage!" Hannah looked pained. "You and Max have the life every one of us aspires to."

"Well, none of you should do that!" Steph's voice wobbled.

She sucked in a shaky breath as Hannah's words hit a nerve that was a lot more sensitive, thanks to her pregnancy. Steph took in a deep breath, trying to gain control of her wayward emotion, but to her mortification, she couldn't and burst into tears.

"Steph!" Hannah said, startled by her sister's reaction. "What's the matter?"

"Do you know how hard it is to live up to everyone's expectations of what my life appears to be?" Steph wailed. "Mine and Max's marriage isn't perfect. In fact, I'm not even sure if we still have a marriage."

She hated herself for no longer being able to keep all her emotions to herself. But it was too late to stop the flood even if she could. Even if she did try to back pedal and make up an excuse for her outburst, Hannah was far too shrewd to let the matter go.

"Steph, what is going on?" Hannah quickly recovered from the shock of Steph's outburst and put her arm around her shoulders. "Please, talk to me."

"What do you want me to say?" Steph sobbed.

"How about starting with what's going on with you and Max," Hannah encouraged.

"After he was injured in that fire two years ago, Max withdrew," Steph admitted. "He started to push me away and to change."

"He went through a lot," Hannah said gently. "Nearly dying, especially in such a traumatic way, will change a person."

"He refuses to talk about or to let anyone in," Steph told her. "He has a lot of trouble sleeping, and when he does sleep, he has nightmares. I've asked him on a few occasions what his dreams were about, but he says he can't remember them." She wiped away her tears. "He refused to admit he has a problem. When we were in the Bahamas, he refused to take off his shirt even when we were doing water sports or sunbathing."

"I know Max is sensitive about his scars." Hannah gave Steph a supportive squeeze. "It does take people who've been disfigured time to accept what's happened to them and come to terms with how it's changed them."

"But will he ever do that if he refuses to admit he has a problem and seeks help?" Steph voiced one of her fears.

"What about *romantic* issues?" Hannah asked as delicately as she could.

"We've hardly been *romantic* at all since he got a clean bill of health," Steph admitted. "It was only while we were in the Bahamas that our *romantic* life sort of sparked back to life." She sighed resignedly. "While we were there, it was as if we had no problems at all. But as soon as we got home, we slipped right back into the pattern we'd been following since the fire."

"Have you told him how you feel?" Hannah asked.

"Maxi is so busy with the Marine center that I hardly see him, and when he's not busy, I'm busy with either the twins or the hotel," Steph informed her.

"You two didn't try to talk about all this while on vacation?" Hannah looked at Steph inquiringly.

"No!" Steph shook her head. "We were too busy having a good time and recapturing our romance."

"In other words, you were both avoiding the subject," Hannah guessed. "Sweeping your problems under the rug and dancing on it, hoping you wouldn't trip on them."

"That's one way of putting it, I guess." Steph's brows raised. "We were having a good time, and I don't think either of us wanted to spoil it by bringing up our problems."

"Wow!" Hannah looked surprised. "You and Max must be the world's best performers because I had no idea you were having problems." She looked at Steph questioningly. "Do the twins know?"

"Gosh, no!" Steph said emphatically. "While Max and I may not have spoken about or admitted to our problems, we have a silent understanding that they stay *our* problems."

"While it is commendable of both of you to keep your kids out of it," Hannah pointed out, "you both need to tell someone, or you will implode." She indicated with a hand at Steph. "Like you're doing now."

"I'm sorry, Han," Steph apologized while Hannah stood and got the box of tissues off the dresser, offering the box to Steph before sitting back on the bed. "I didn't mean to gush all over you."

"Don't be silly." Hannah waved her off. "I'm here for you no matter what."

"I'm glad," Steph said, blowing her nose. "Because I think I need to speak to someone about all this." She hiccupped. "Especially since I think Max is having an affair."

"WHAT?" Hannah got such a shock she nearly choked on the air she breathed in.

"And on top of that," Steph said, taking a deep breath and getting ready to drop the next bombshell on her younger sister. "I'm eight weeks pregnant, which is the real reason I collapsed yesterday."

This time, Hannah did choke upon hearing the news. "Oh, Steph!"

"And the reason I needed space from my life back on Marco Island and Max is because I have no idea what I'm going to do about the pregnancy or Max!" Steph burst into tears once again. Hannah wrapped her arms around Steph and let her cry.

CHAPTER 6

Max wandered aimlessly through the empty pool house. His heart was heavy as his mind played the fight with Steph on repeat. He checked his phone once again, but she still hadn't replied to his message, and all Max wanted to do was call her to work things out. But he understood—or at least he was trying to—understand that Steph needed space. Max knew he shouldn't have suspected her of having an affair, but things had not been stable in their relationship for the past two years.

Max ran a hand warily over his face as he stood in the kitchen, staring at the closed refrigerator. Seeing Steph in another man's arms felt like he'd been punched in the stomach and stabbed in the heart. It was a couple of hours after the fight when he realized how jealous and suspicious he was being. The feeling was a foreign one to Max as he never was a jealous person and always gave people the benefit of the doubt. He firmly believed that everyone needed to be given a chance to explain themselves—at least, he used to be.

Max pulled a bottle of water from the refrigerator and remembered that Wallis had invited him over to watch a game. While Max wasn't really in the mood for company, he also didn't want to mope around an empty house. He got his phone and called Wallis.

"Hey!" Wallis answered after the fifth ring.

"Hi, Steph and the kids have gone to Palm Beach for a few days, so if the invitation is still open..." Max didn't get to finish his sentence.

"Of course it is," Walls assured him. "You caught me just in time as I was deciding what to order for dinner."

"Great!" Max said. "I'll be over in fifteen minutes, and we can decide then."

When they'd hung up, Max went to change out of his work clothes before heading out to Wallis's. He almost changed his mind about going twice as he drove to his friend's house, but as soon as Max arrived, he was glad he hadn't. It was good for him to get out, and the two of them hadn't hung out for a while. It was also the first time both of their wives and kids were away. They ordered burgers and settled in to watch the game.

After their team won, they went out onto the deck. The two friends kicked back in their chairs, sipping their cold beers. The night had fully descended, casting a serene, almost magical ambiance over Wallis's lakefront property. The moon, a silvery orb in the vast canvas of the night sky, was now high above the horizon. Its shimmering light bathed the world below in a soft, ethereal glow. The lake curved beside them, glistening beneath the tender moonlight caress like a sea of liquid silver.

A warm breeze rustled the leaves of nearby palm trees, creating a soothing lullaby that harmonized with the rhythmic chirping of crickets. The world felt at peace, a quiet symphony of nature's wonders playing out around them. Max and Wallis sat in companionable silence, their words replaced by the gentle night sounds and the play of moonlight on the water.

In that serene moment, Max's troubles hit pause at the back of his mind as he enjoyed the tranquil beauty of the world around them. He was glad he'd decided to visit Wallis. Max had needed a couple of hours with nothing but the simplicity of lifelong friendship, shared laughter, and the absorbing excitement of watching a ballgame.

"This is a first for us," Wallis broke the silence.

"We've watched ballgames together before," Max teased while knowing what Wallis meant.

He glanced at his friend, and it wasn't the first time that night he'd noticed a wariness etched with a tinge of sadness in Wallis's eyes. Max frowned, wondering if everything was okay. On the surface, Wallis had seemed to be his usually cheerful self, but Max had felt an underlying current as if his cheerfulness was only surface-deep. At first, Max had thought he'd been projecting his own doubt, hurt, and sorrow onto his friend.

"Yeah, but this time's different!" Wallis sipped his beer and stared out over the lake.

"Do you mean because our wives and kids are away?" Max decided to tread lightly and let Wallis steer the conversation.

"Yes," Wallis acknowledged and turned toward Max. "Heather and I are taking some time apart to decide if we still want to be married."

That's a blunt way of putting it! Max thought, his eyes widening in shock as he stared at his friend. "What?" He shook his head, making sure he'd heard his friend correctly. "What's going on?"

"It's my fault." Wallis's voice dropped with his head as he looked at his beer bottle and picked at the label. "The promotion to VP at work took over my life, and my family, especially Heather, felt I cared more about my job than them."

"How long has this been going on?" Max watched Wallis intently.

"Two years!" Wallis gave a self-mocking laugh. "I was so wrapped up in my work that I didn't even notice my family slipping away from me."

"No way!" Max was astounded.

He'd never have guessed Wallis and Heather were having problems. They always seemed so happy and in sync.

"I'm afraid so!" Wallis sighed deeply. "I worked so hard to ensure my family had a good life that I turned the good life into a miserable one by never being around to enjoy it with them," Wallis confessed, his voice tinged with regret.

Max nodded, the moonlight catching the somber expression on his friend's face. "You know, Wallis, it's a common trap. We get so caught up in providing for our loved ones, in building this perfect life for them, that we forget the most important part–being there with them. We become so focused on the destination that we forget the journey, and in the end, it's the moments we shared, the time we spent with them, that matter the most."

Wallis took a deep swig of his beer. "You're right. Only I woke up a little too late, and Heather had one foot out the door with the kids." He shook his head. "All the missed family dinners, the canceled vacations, and the late nights at the office... I thought I was doing it for them, but Heather's right." He snorted. "It stopped being about the good life when I exceeded that goal and went into excess." He took another sip, pausing as he swallowed. "The higher I climbed, the more I had, the more I wanted, and the higher I wanted to get." He pinched the bridge of his nose. "Until eventually, I rose to the top, leaving my family to fend for themselves. I missed out on so much by not being there."

Max placed a reassuring hand on Wallis's shoulder. "Hopefully, it's not too late to make a change, my friend." He gave Wallis a reassuring smile. "It's time to shift gears, to find that balance between work and family. To create more of those moments, you won't want to miss."

Wallis pursed his lips and bounced his brows. "I've already resigned from the law firm and have taken a position with my parent's small family law firm." He peeled off what was left of the label on his bottle. "I won't have to commute to Naples every day because, as you know, my father's law firm is right here on Marco Island." He shrugged. "And the hours are way better." He looked at Max. "We have enough saved up to live comfortably right through retirement, and Heather wants to return to teaching at Marco Island High School."

"Oh, wow, that's awesome, Wallis," Max said, and they chinked beer bottles. "Your parents must be pleased. I know they've wanted you to work with them."

"Yeah, they're thrilled." Wallis nodded. "So are the kids. When I work there, and they stop by my parent's after school, I'll be there too."

"Surely Heather must be thrilled as well?" Max asked.

"She's happy that I've taken a step toward trying to mend the family," Wallis replied. "But our relationship still needs work, and she wants us to see a marriage counselor."

"That's not so bad," Max assured him. "I've heard it can be really good for a marriage."

"Or really bad when you eventually open up and are shocked to find all the truths your partner has been storing up through the relationship." Wallis gave a soft laugh.

"There's always that side of it, too," Max agreed. "But it's better to get it all out than let it fester and turn what was once a beautiful relationship into an ugly one full of hurt, hate, and regret."

"True!" Wallis nodded in agreement. "Heather has already enlightened me with a lot of truths that I hadn't even noticed about our marriage."

"I'm sure if you look deep enough, you'll find you're harboring a lot of things you've been unhappy with or didn't agree with about the marriage as well," Max pointed out.

"I guess." Wallis shrugged. "I guess I always tried to see my grievances from Heather's point of view."

"Now that's the lawyer in you!" Max laughed, then patted Wallis's heart. "You need to speak from your heart on all matters even if you know Heather won't like or agree with it." Max raised his eyebrows. "Or even if you know they may hurt her because if you go to a therapist, they are going to dig those same grievances out of Heather too."

"I know!" Wallis blew out a breath. "I love her so darn much that I would never want to hurt like that."

"But, Wallis, you've hurt her unintentionally by trying to do what you thought was right by her and your family!" Max listened to his friend, his heart going out for him.

Max looked over the river as he realized the similarities between their marriage situations. Steph told him they needed space and then put one hundred and twenty-five miles between them. Max had basically accused her of having an affair and acted like a jealous teenager. If the roles had been reversed, he'd probably also want to put some space between them. But Max wouldn't have gone to another town. He'd probably have checked into a hotel for a few nights until Steph had calmed down and they could talk rationally.

"Hey, buddy, are you okay?" Wallis asked with a frown as he looked worriedly at Max. "You look like someone just stole your lunch or something."

"Not my lunch." Max took in a breath. "But I did think someone was trying to steal my wife earlier today."

"What?" Wallis spluttered. "Do you mean, like, kidnap her?" He turned his face slightly. "Or steal her romantically?"

"Romantically," Max clarified. "I went to find Steph at the hotel this morning and found her in the arms of Tom Barnes."

"Ah!" Wallis nodded in understanding. "That's why you were asking me questions about Tom today."

"Yeah." Max snorted as he realized how absurd he was being. "The worst part was that I asked Steph if she was having an affair with him."

"No!" Wallis gaped at Max before frowning and asking. "Why was she in Tom's arms?"

"I don't know." Max shook his head. "Steph never told me in between throwing her car keys at me, telling me to search all her messages, etcetera, and then storming out of the house."

"I hope the kids weren't home to hear all this?" Wallis said.

"No, they'd gone surfing," Max told him. "I went to work thinking Steph and I would sort it out when I got home from work only to find an empty house and note telling me Steph, the boys, and Tammy had gone to Palm Beach with Hannah."

"Wow!" Wallis gave a low whistle. "Looks like we are in similar boats, not knowing which paddle to use to get us home."

"You've got that right." Max held up the bottle in a saluting acknowledgment. "Thank you for inviting me over tonight, or I'd be a miserable heap moping on my couch."

"That would've made two of us." Wallis frowned curiously. "I know before you went to the Bahamas, you said that you felt like you and Steph had been drifting apart since the fire. We haven't had much time to talk since then. Were things getting better between the two of you before today's blow-up?"

"Steph and I had the most amazing time in the Bahamas." Max lifted his ankle over his knee. "We rekindle our old spark that burned so bright before the fire."

"Maybe burn so bright isn't the best analogy to use in the same sentence as before the fire," Wallis pointed out with a grin, trying to lighten the mood.

"True." Max laughed. "But as soon as we got back from the Bahamas, the trip became a distant memory the moment we stepped foot on Marco Island."

"You know, seeing the two of you together, not even your close family or friends know you're having problems," Wallis commented. "You both always seem so happy and together."

"I was thinking the same about you and Heather," Max remarked. "I guess the saying that nothing is usually ever as it seems is true." He shook his head. "You told me yours and Heather's problems started two years ago." He pulled a face. "So, did mine and Steph's."

"That would've been right after the fire you got injured in," Wallis remembered. "Geez, buddy, that was stressful on all of us, especially on your wife and father. It was touch and go for you."

"I know!" Max's voice became hoarse with emotion as images of the fire flashed through his mind, and the raw scars on his body stung as he could still feel the flames scorching his skin with its fiery touch. "I was so consumed with guilt and physical pain when I was eventually released from hospital that I pushed Steph away."

"You've never spoken about what happened in the fire or how you were injured," Wallis pointed out. "I never wanted to ask, as I figured you'd tell me when you were ready."

"I haven't told anyone." Max put his empty beer bottle on the table in front of them. "It's not a day I want to remember, let alone tell anyone about."

"You saved a woman from a house fire!" Wallis raised his brows. "You're a hero, my friend. I know you got severely injured. But not many people would rush into a burning house on their day off without all your protective gear."

"Rescuing people from fire and fighting it is what I was trained for. It was my job. My calling," Max told him. "I wouldn't call myself a hero for doing my job."

"But you were off duty," Wallis stressed. "And completely unprepared to come across a fire while on your morning run."

"I'm a firefighter. We're always prepared for fires," Max commented. "Just because I didn't have the uniform on that day didn't make me any less of a firefighter."

"No, it made you a hero!" Wallis insisted. "An insane one, but a hero nonetheless."

Max laughed and shook his head at his stubborn friend.

"Are you ready to tell me what happened?" Wallis put his empty bottle next to Max's and sat back, staring at Max expectantly. "Or at least just the basic bits about how you came across the fire or why you were running near the marine center that day. Your usual route is along Tigertail beach."

"As you know, the twins and I started volunteering at the Marine Center over the weekends. It was a nice activity for the three of us to do together," Max explained. "Three weekends before the fire, one of the other volunteers at the center gave me a flier. It was for a fun run to raise money for the center."

"Yes, I remember that run," Wallis told him. "It nearly got canceled after the fire because the run went past the house that burned down."

"When the runners signed up, they got given a map with the route." Max rubbed the back of his neck. "I started practicing along the route every morning and night depending on when I was on duty." He pulled his ankle, which was resting on his knee, further up his leg. "When I ran past the house that burned on the way toward the center, the house was fine. There wasn't a hint of smoke. But twenty minutes later, when I was running home, I could smell the smoke a distance away and the screams."

"You, being the man and firefighter that you are, naturally rushed right into the flames to save the person trapped in the house without a moment's hesitation," Wallis added what he guessed happened to the story.

"I did what I was trained to do," Max continued. "I called the emergency services as I raced toward the house. When I saw the state the house was in and determined which side of it the screams were coming from, I took my shirt off to use as a mask and made my way as cautiously as I could into the house."

"Geez, Max." Wallis looked at him wide-eyed.

"I found the woman cowering in the corner of one of the rooms, unable to move in fear," Max's mind went back to that day, and he could still see the look of terror in her eyes. "I went to her and managed to get her to move. As we neared the front door, a beam collapsed, and I shielded her with my body, catching some of the flames that jumped from the beams."

"That's how that side of your body got burned," Wallis realized.

Max nodded in confirmation. "A beam had also collapsed, blocking our exit through the front door. I had no option but to move it with my bare hands." He held up his palms. The scars seemed to look brighter in the dark. "I managed to push the woman out as another beam collapsed."

"Only this time, it collapsed on you!" Wallis knew that part of the story and shuddered as he remembered it being told them when they'd gone to the hospital. "You were lucky the firefighters got there just in time."

"Trust me, that plays over and over in my mind." Max swallowed and shut his eyes as the images of that beam collapsing on him flooded his mind. He opened his eyes and stared at the shimmering river. "I keep thinking, what if they were a minute later?"

"You are really lucky to be alive, my friend." Wallis patted Max's shoulder. "Maybe you and Steph should consider going to a marriage counselor, too." He bit the side of his mouth thoughtfully. "Or at least get yourself some therapy, as you're still haunted by what happened that day."

"I feel better now that I've told you!" Max looked at Wallis.

"Yeah, but I'm not a therapist. I'm just your friend sitting here and listening," Wallis pointed out. "You need someone that can help you face and get rid of your ghosts."

"I don't know." Max shrugged. "I think you're doing a great job helping me by just listening and *not* trying to fix something that I don't think can be fixed by anything but time." He smiled. "Besides. I'm fine, and I feel I've managed to get over it since I started working at the Marine Center."

"Max, it's been two years, and I could see in your eyes that it still feels like it happened a day ago to you," Wallis observed. "You forget, my friend, that we've been best buds from before we could walk. I know you and know you're anything but fine and nowhere near over what happened."

"Now you're starting to sound like Steph and my father," Max told him, and at the mention of her name, his heart squeezed painfully, and his features dropped. "But I think you're right about Steph and I trying therapy."

"As you told me, it could be a great help even if things get stormy and we hear things we don't like or cut us to the bone." Wallis looked at his wristwatch. "It's getting late. Why don't you stay the night? The guest bedroom is made up."

"Thanks, I'll do that," Max accepted the offer. "It will be better than going home to an empty house."

"Trust me, the first night is the worst and loneliest." Wallis stood and collected the empty bottle. He turned and frowned. "Did you know who the woman was that you saved? I know that she wasn't supposed to be in that house. But that's all anyone knows, as her name was never mentioned."

"I didn't know her," Max answered Wallis. "But I had met her about two months before the fire. She'd gotten a flat tire on the road out of Marco Island, and I stopped to help her."

Max frowned when he saw the astonished look on Wallis's face.

"Are you kidding me?" Wallis gaped at Max. "The woman who kept sending you chocolates, flowers, and notes to the fire station?" He gave his head a shake as if he thought he'd heard Max wrong.

"She was thankful that I helped her." Max shrugged, unsure why Wallis was making a big deal out of it. "She only sent three boxes of chocolates, and the notes were attached to them. It was because she was grateful that I was instrumental in getting her to a job interview on time."

"No, Max." Wallis's voice lowered. "It wasn't only those notes she sent to the station." He stared at Max. "Luckily, I'm not breaking any lawyer-client privilege as my father took over the case."

"What are you talking about?" Cold fingers started to walk up Max's spine at the way Wallis's voice had lowered, and his eyes had narrowed. That was Wallis's, *I'm about to drop a bombshell on you,* look.

"The woman you helped on the side of the road started stalking Steph!" Wallis's words floored Max, and the cold fingers closed around his heart. "To the extent that my father had to threaten her with a restraining order. Just to make sure the woman heeded the warning, my father made sure the woman's father, who is also a prominent Marco Island figure wanting to run as the next mayor, got the memo." His eyebrows rose. "So, you can imagine all our surprise when you hired her to work at the Marine Center recently."

"What?" Max choked. "Kendal was stalking Steph?"

CHAPTER 7

It had been two days since Steph and the teens had been in Palm Beach with Hannah. The twins and Tammy were having a great time, but Steph couldn't relax. Her mind was racked with guilt over not having told Max she was pregnant. Then, there was the constant worry that Steph had given him even more space to be with Kendal. On top of that, there was the crushing stress and anxiety over having not resolved the first huge blow-up she and Max had ever had. Steph hated the thought that she'd left him wondering if she was having an affair with Tom.

"He's the one having an affair!" Steph muttered as she pulled on a summer dress in her room. She'd just had her morning shower and was about to head downstairs to join her family for breakfast. "Or is possibly having an affair." She corrected herself. "You don't know that for certain, Steph." She slipped on her sandals. "Innocent until caught in the act."

Steph pulled the bedroom door open and, thanks to her quick reflexes, managed to narrowly avoid being punched in the face as Hannah was about to knock on the door.

"Oh, shucks, sorry, Steph!" Hannah's eyes rounded as she dropped her hand.

"Didn't you hear me opening the door?" Steph stood staring at her sister.

"No. My mind was far away," Hannah admitted.

Steph frowned as something flashed in her sister's eyes. It was the same look of confusion and uncertainty that had been there the other day when they were discussing Hannah's relationship with her fiancé.

"Is everything okay?" Steph asked Hannah with concern.

"I'm fine," Hannah tried to reassure Steph. "Just work stuff."

Steph knew her sister far too well to be fooled by Hannah saying *I'm fine*. It usually meant she wasn't, but Hannah didn't want anyone prying. Steph wasn't going to push her, but she would try and subtly get it out of Hannah what was bothering her.

"I thought you were on another break from work?" Steph followed Hannah downstairs.

"I am," Hannah confirmed before changing the subject. "Have you decided whether to hire a car and drive back to Marco Island today?"

"I am going to." Steph nodded. "Are you sure it's okay to leave Liam, Jack, and Tammy with you for a week?"

"Of course," Hannah said. "I'm going to love having them here, and I promise I'll take excellent care of them. I've already cleared it with Lorry for Tammy to be here without you."

"Oh?" Steph's eyes widened. "You spoke to Lorry?"

"I called her this morning," Hannah told her and smiled. "Don't worry, I didn't tell her why you were going home. I told her I thought it would be a nice break for you and Max, and Lorry agreed."

"Thank you, Han." Steph hugged her sister. "I'm sorry to make you keep my secret about my failing marriage, and you know what else." She touched her stomach.

"Of course." Hannah squeezed Steph's arm. "That's your news to tell my sister, not mine."

They walked into the kitchen, where the teenagers were finishing their breakfast. Steph was greeted by a chorus of good mornings and hugs before she settled at the breakfast table and helped herself to some granola.

"What are you three up to today?" Steph asked the teens.

"Aunt Hannah said we could go horseback riding and then surfing," Liam answered for them.

"That sounds like fun," Steph said, grinning at their happy faces.

"Do you want to come with us, Aunt Steph?" Tammy asked her.

"No, thanks, honey," Steph declined and looked around the table. "I need to get back to Marco Island to deal with some hotel stuff." She lied. "Last night, Hannah agreed that the three of you can stay here with her for another week if you want to."

"YES!" Liam, Jack, and Tammy chorused happily.

"I guess that settles that!" Hannah laughed and looked at Tammy. "Don't worry, Tammy. I've already spoken to your mom, and she's happy for you to stay with just me."

"Thanks, Aunt Hannah." Tammy sighed in relief. "Mom can be a pain when it comes to who I stay with."

"She's only looking out for you, love," Steph told her.

Tammy nodded and finished her toast before turning to the twins. "Should we go to the stables and wait there for Aunt Hannah?"

"Yeah, great idea, Tam," Liam said.

"Do you mind, Aunt Hannah?" Jack, always the responsible one, asked.

"Of course," Hannah told him. "Tell Ryan, the stable manager, that I sent you to choose horses, and I'll be along as soon as I've dropped your mother at the car rental." She looked at Steph. "It's only five minutes up the road."

"I can walk," Steph said.

"No!" Hannah shook her head emphatically. "You *cannot*."

"I agree with Aunt Hannah, Mom," Jack backed Hannah up. "You were ill the other day, and you could faint again along the way."

"Fine!" Steph hugged Jack. "I know when I'm beaten. I'll let Hannah drive me."

The twins and Tammy finished their breakfast, and after saying goodbye to Steph, they headed out the back door and toward the stables at the end of Hannah's garden.

"I'm going to miss them," Steph noted as she watched the three teenagers disappear through the gate at the end of the yard.

"This is going to be good for you and Max." Hannah reached over and squeezed Steph's hand. "You two need to sort things out, and this way, you do it without the stress of being careful that the twins don't hear you."

"I know." Steph sighed and sat back in the seat, sipping ginger tea.

"I am worried about you driving for two and a half hours alone," Hannah admitted.

"I'll be fine." Steph put on a brave smile. "Besides, the drive will give me a lot of time to think things through, so when I get home, I'll have a level head and hopefully know what I want to say to Max."

"And you're going to tell him about—" Hannah glanced pointedly at Steph's stomach.

"I will," Steph assured her sister. "Thank you again for looking after the twins and Tammy to give us this space."

"I love having my niece and nephews here," Hannah told her. "I can't wait to get to a stage when I can have Riley with me too."

"Do you think Nicky will ever let her daughter out of her sight long enough to visit you?" They laughed.

"I'm sure Nicky will learn to let go eventually," Hannah said. "She's only been a mom for a couple of months now, and Riley is not even two months old yet."

The mention of their older sister Nicky's baby made Steph's mind whirl once more as her own pregnancy was still waiting for her to decide what to do. She pushed her thoughts to the back of her mind and went to get ready for her drive home.

An hour later, Steph was on the road in a rental car and heading home to Marco Island. She hadn't told Max she was coming home, and Hannah would tell the twins not to either, as Steph wanted to surprise him. Guilt surged through her because Steph knew she didn't want to surprise Max in a good way—she was trying to catch him out so she'd know once and for all if he was cheating on her.

The road from Palm Beach to Marco Island stretched before her like a ribbon of possibilities. The route was familiar, etched in her memory after so many trips back and forth. The early morning sun cast a warm, golden hue on the landscape, illuminating the road as it meandered through South Florida's coastal beauty.

As the miles rolled by, Steph's thoughts drifted back two years to that evening when Max had returned from his firefighting course in Naples. The memories of that night were etched in her heart, a stark contrast to the uncertainty and unease that filled her mind today.

In the warm evening air, Max had walked into their home, his face flushed with excitement and a hint of exhaustion from the long day. He'd dropped his gear by the door and pulled Steph into a tight embrace. They'd held each other for a long moment, basking in the happiness of being together.

Max had spoken animatedly about the course and how he had helped a woman with a flat tire on his way back, which was why he'd been late getting home. It was just another testament to his caring nature. Steph had listened with rapt attention as he detailed the events, his eyes sparkling enthusiastically.

Then, his voice had lowered, taking on a more serious tone. Max revealed that he was currently in top position to become the new and youngest Marco Island fire captain in a year after the current captain retired.

The excitement in Max's eyes had been contagious, and Steph had felt her heart swell with pride for her husband. She'd known how much the position meant to him, the chance to lead his team, and the opportunity to make a difference in the community.

With their twin sons, who were twelve at the time, they'd gone out to dinner to celebrate. Laughter had filled the restaurant as they toasted to Max's achievements and shared future dreams. It was a night of love, hope, and unwavering support for each other, starkly contrasting the emotional turmoil that had unfolded with the events yet to come.

As Steph continued to drive along the scenic route, she couldn't help but long for the days when their love was unwavering and those dreams were still intact. Suddenly, the road ahead seemed to stretch infinitely, much like the uncertainty in her heart. Steph swallowed the lump that was burning her throat and pushing tears to her eyes.

While their family was celebrating Max's future, little did they know that one act of chivalry was about to threaten their happiness and put a strain on their small, tightly-knit family. A week after that night, a woman in her early thirties had knocked on their front door when Max was on duty at the fire station.

Steph had answered it, and thank goodness the twins had been with her mother when Kendal James introduced herself as the woman Max had saved a week ago. She'd brought him a heart-shaped box of chocolates and one of Max's T-shirts.

The road in front of Steph faded away to that night.

Two Years Ago - two months before the fire

Steph had been getting ready to climb into a relaxing bubble bath when a knock at the door seemed to resound through the empty house. Muttering to herself, she pulled on her robe and slippers, then headed downstairs to answer it. Her brow knit into a tight frown when she saw a woman who seemed familiar standing there.

The woman's eyes widened in surprise when Steph answered the door.

"Oh!" The woman said. "I'm sorry, I was looking for Max."

"My *husband*, Max, isn't here at the moment," Steph answered, warning bells ringing in her head. There was something about the way the woman had said Max's name that had made her hackles rise.

"Your husband?" The woman's frown deepened. "I'm sorry, there must be some mistake. I met Max the other night, and he said nothing about a wife."

Steph looked at the woman, a mixture of confusion and suspicion in her gaze. She couldn't quite articulate her feelings, but her instincts told her something was amiss.

"Excuse me?" Steph's hand on the front door tightened as she held it slightly closed.

"This is awkward," The woman said, and Steph didn't see anything to indicate the woman felt awkward or even slightly embarrassed to be talking to Steph after implying what she was. "I wanted to give these chocolates to Max as he came to my rescue the other night, and after that, we met for ice cream. While strolling along the beach, I got wet, and he loaned me his shirt." She shoved the items at Steph.

"Oh?" Steph's eyebrows rose in disbelief as she stared at the woman. "Are you the woman he changed the flat tire for?"

"Yes." The woman nodded. "And he gave me his number and called me a few nights ago to meet for an ice cream."

"Really?" Steph let go of the door and folded her arms. Her heart was hammering in her chest. "What night was this?"

"Friday night." The woman said unapologetically.

She seemed utterly unphased that she was telling Max's wife they'd met for a date. Steph actually thought the woman was enjoying the upset she thought she was causing.

What kind of person is she? Steph thought, dumbfounded by the woman's audacity.

Then, another thought struck Steph. Max was at work on Friday night, and they had a bush fire on the outskirts of town that the fire department had attended, which took nearly the entire shift to get under control.

"Are you sure it was Friday?" Steph didn't know what game the woman was playing but refused to be drawn into it.

Steph threw the chocolates in the trash can beside the front door, ensuring the woman saw what she'd done before holding up the T-shirt. Steph noticed it looked brand new and was about two sizes too small for Max. Plus, he never wore brown.

"Of course I am." The woman's eyes narrowed, and a flash of anger flitted through them when she watched Steph throw away the chocolates. "You can't do that. Those are for Max."

"My *husband* doesn't eat chocolates," Steph pointed out. "Even if he did eat ice cream, which Max doesn't as he has a dairy intolerance, I know he was attending to a fire outside of town on Friday night." She shook her head as her own anger sparked. "I don't know what kind of game you're playing here." She shoved the shirt back at the woman. "But this is not Max's shirt, and please don't darken our doorstep again."

Steph went to push the door shut, but the woman put her foot through it, stopping her.

"Max lied to you about where he was on Friday night." The woman's voice resonated with anger. "He wants you out of his life so we can be together."

"What?" Steph gaped at the woman in utter disbelief. "Are you delusional?"

"No, but you are!" The woman stepped up to Steph, looming in the doorway so Steph couldn't shut the door in her face. "I'm warning you to back off and leave so Max and I can be together."

Steph pulled her phone from her pocket. She tried to steady her shaking hands as she dialed 9-1-1. The woman was clearly unstable, and Steph was feeling unsafe with her standing in her doorway.

"Yes, call Max," the woman challenged. "If he doesn't know how to get rid of you, I'll show I can."

"What is wrong with you?" Steph breathed as emergency services answered. "Hello." She tried to keep her voice steady while never taking her eyes off the angry woman in her doorway. "Please, can you send a police car to my address as I have an intruder?"

"You called the police?" The woman's eyes widened, and her anger turned to fear. "Please, hang up. I'll leave."

Steph ignored the woman and gave the emergency services her address. The operator stayed on the line with Steph as she explained what was happening.

"She's lying," the woman screeched when Steph told the operator that the woman was delusional and was stalking Max.

The woman tried to grab the phone from Steph, but Steph managed to dodge her and was about to run into the living room to lock herself in when a siren sounded in her driveway, and flashing lights lit up the hallway.

"You're going to pay for this!" the woman hissed as two officers rushed inside.

"Miss James?" The police officer looked at the intruder in surprise.

"This is all a terrible misunderstanding!" Miss James told the officers, but the senior one didn't seem to care who Miss James was and cuffed her.

The senior office watched the other one lead Miss James from the house.

"You're going to pay for this!" Miss James shouted at Steph.

"I'm sorry about this," the office told Steph before taking her statement. "Look, I'm not going to lie to you. Kendal James won't even make it to lock up, and her father will have her bailed out."

"James?" Steph frowned at the surname. "As in Bruno James? The prominent businessman who is running for mayor?"

"Yes." The officer nodded. "Kendal is his only child."

Something occurred to Steph. "When you saw her, you didn't seem surprised that I'd reported her."

"I was just about to warn you about her," the officer told Steph. "It's not her first stalking offense." He started walking toward the front door. "Please be careful. She'll probably back off now as she didn't get to intimidate you, but just watch out for her."

"Thank you, officer," Steph walked him to the door and saw him out.

Once the police car had driven off, Steph allowed herself to give in to her fear and felt as if she'd been trapped in a bad dream. It all felt so unreal. After ensuring every window was shut, and the doors were locked, Steph finally got to freshen her bath and climb in, letting the soothing bubble water soak away the fear. Only the doubt that had crept in and hidden behind was left behind, stuck in her mind.

The following two weeks became a silent nightmare for Steph. She'd asked Max about Kendal James, and he'd told her she'd sent him some chocolates and thank-you notes for saving her. Max had fobbed it off as Kendal being grateful that Max had helped her get to an interview on time.

Steph had wondered what interview she'd be having in the evening but had let the matter go. She hadn't told Max about the incident at the house as he'd been so busy at work. The station captain had a heart attack two days after Max's Naples course had finished. As second in command, Max had stepped in as acting captain.

Three days after Steph had gotten Kendal taken away from the house by the police, she'd started getting threatening text message boxes of dead roses sent to the hotel for Steph. On numerous occasions, Steph would walk home and catch glimpses of Kendal lurking around. Then, one night, Max was in the shower when Steph saw a message from Kendal flash up on Max's phone.

Hey handsome, we're having a party at the Marine Center, you should come join us.

Steph had gone cold, and her heart felt like it had dropped to her feet. Max hadn't mentioned that Kendal was associated with the Marine Center, and the doubt had flooded in. Steph had asked Max, and he'd confirmed that Kendal also volunteered there as she was a qualified marine biologist, just like Max was. Suspicion had been born in Steph's mind that night, and she had a horrible feeling that Kendal was dangerous.

Max didn't think anything of Kendal appearing wherever they were or that she seemed to like and do everything Max did. Whenever Max was out surfing with the twins or at the Marine Center volunteering, Kendal would send Steph a message letting her know how much fun she and Max were having. When Steph tried to broach the subject of Kendal being obsessed with Max, he'd laugh Steph off and tease her about being jealous before letting her know that no one could replace Steph in his heart—Kendal was just a friend.

Steph was left in a situation where she didn't want to come across as the jealous, mistrustful wife, but the doubt and suspicion were setting in more and more. She did her best to ignore and brush Kendal's taunting's aside until, one day, Steph had stayed at her parent's house to look after her gran. When she got home the following day, she saw Kendal leaving the house in one of Max's shirts.

Steph had taken a photo of Kendal sneaking out of the house, and when she'd gone, Steph had rushed inside, but Max wasn't home. That was the first time she'd called one of his firefighters to find out if Max had been at the station the entire night. The firefighter had assured Steph he had been and hadn't left. It had left Steph feeling unsafe, and she'd known that Kendal had been watching her. That's when Steph knew she could no longer keep what was happening to herself and had called Wallis for help.

Wallis and his father took over the case, and Kendal's harassment stopped. She disappeared for over a year and returned ten months ago after getting a position as a marine biologist at the Marine Center. While Kendal no longer harassed Steph, the woman made subtle hints at her relationship with Max, using Clyde as her tool to deliver the messages. Clyde didn't know he was Kendal's pawn, and Steph suspected he was in love with the horrid woman. When he griped to Steph about how Kendal followed Max around like a puppy, he did so out of jealousy as she wasn't paying him the same attention.

Present Day

Before Steph realized it, she was driving into Marco Island, and her heart started thumping against her chest as she neared home. As she passed hers and Max's house that was being renovated, something made her stop. She pulled up, parked the car, and walked through the front gate. As she stepped through, she froze, and her eyes widened as her breath caught in her throat.

She felt like she was glued to the spot as she watched the scene she dreaded most play out in front of her eyes. Max and Kendal stood near the front door. His back was to the gate as his attention was glued to Kendal and hadn't noticed Steph standing at the gate. Before she could call him Steph's eyes collided with Kendal's. Kendal's lips curled into a smirk as she looked smugly at Steph, then turned to Max and plastered her lips to his.

Steph felt like she'd been impaled through the heart with a dagger of betrayal as Max's arms shot out, and his hand gripped Kendal's arms. Anger, hurt, jealousy, and a host of other emotions Steph couldn't identify flooded through her.

Before she could stop herself, she shouted, "And you accused *me* of having an affair."

Before waiting for Max to realize she was there, Steph turned and fled. As she pulled off in her rental car, tears streamed down her face, and she drove off.

CHAPTER 8

Max had been so excited to be able to help put the finishing touches on his and Steph's house. It was finally finished, and when Steph and the twins got home, they could move in within a few days. Max couldn't wait. While he loved his in-laws and extended family, he loved his own home, and he knew the boys, and Steph missed it as much as he did. But the storm damage from the previous year had forced them to evacuate and for the house to undergo repairs, which presented them with the perfect opportunity to renovate it as they had planned for the future.

Max was finishing giving the bathroom in his and Steph's bedroom its final clean when the doorbell had rung. He'd been surprised to see Kendal there with Chinese take-out and coffee. While Max was still trying to make sense of the story Wallis had told him about how Kendal had stalked Steph, he didn't want her to figure out he knew about it. Max wanted to terminate her position at the Marine Center and needed to find a way to do it without looking like she was losing her job due to personal reasons.

Max also didn't want to give Kendal a reason to start stalking and harassing Steph and was also terrified she may extend her harassment to his kids this time. After Wallis had told him about what Kendal had done to Steph, he'd started to realize what Clyde had been warning him about all these months. Kendal was trying to make him see her in a romantic way, but that was never going to happen. While Max and Steph were having a few relationship problems, he would never look at another woman. Steph was the love of his life and his soulmate. There'd be no other for him.

Max had contacted a few other Marine Centers to try and get her relocated to one of them. He had the perfect excuse to do so as soon as the new habitats were completed, and Max had pressured the workers to get them done quicker by bringing up the due date. Instead of them being completed in a month, Max wanted them done within a week, and thankfully, Mike had agreed to help Max with the finances to do it. More workers were starting the next day, and two students studying marine biology would be helping out.

"Max?" Kendal's voice pulled him from his thoughts. "I brought you some food and coffee!" Kendal held up the bag. "Clyde told me you were working on your house today, and as your wife and kids are out of town, I figured you wouldn't have eaten."

"I actually ate at the hotel," Max told her, trying to keep his attitude casual and forcefully stopping himself from kicking her out. He didn't want her inside his family's house. "I've just finished what I was doing here and was heading out."

"Oh!" Kendal tried to look past him into the house. "Maybe one of the contractors could have the food then."

"Sure, I'll have it," Dave, a burly guy who was clearing away the building equipment, was walking past when he heard her offer.

"Here you go," Kendal handed the bag and coffee to Dave, giving him her sweetest smile.

"Aren't you Bruno James's daughter?" Dave asked her, taking a swig of the coffee.

Max watched with interest as Kendal seemed to balk at the mention of her father and realized she was scared of the man.

"Yes, that's right." Kendal nodded.

"Thanks for the food and coffee." Dave walked off.

Kendal turned to Max. "I tried to call you the other night when I heard your wife and kids left you alone." She gave him an alluring smile. "I thought you may want company."

"Nope, I was out." Max didn't elaborate. "I'm sorry, Kendal, but I must get home and wash up as I'm going out with my sister-in-law and her fiancé."

"Where are you going?" Kendal's eyes lit with interest. "Maybe I could meet you there."

"I don't think so," Max said, stepping out of the house and pulling the door closed. "I'll walk you to the gate."

Max started to walk when Kendal stepped off the small step, and her ankle buckled. She reached out for Max, and he automatically grabbed her to steady her. Once she was stable, he quickly let her go.

"Are you okay?" Max asked.

"I'm fine," Kendal told him before his attention was caught by something behind him.

But before Max could turn to see, Kendal grabbed him and plastered her lips to his. Shock paralyzed him for a few seconds before he grabbed her by the arms. Max was about to push Kendal away when Steph's voice shot through him like a whip.

"And you accused *me* of having an affair," Steph shouted from the gate.

Max shoved Kendal away from him so hard that she fell over, but he didn't care. His heart was hammering in his ears as he dashed after Steph, but before he could get to her, she'd roared off in a new car.

Fury burst through Max's veins as he spun on his heels and was about to storm toward Kenda and demand to know if she did that on purpose when he nearly ran her over as she was right behind him.

"Wow, your wife is so volatile!" Kendal said, wide-eyed. "Do you know that a few years ago, she had me arrested for bringing a thank you for helping me gift?"

"Did you know Steph was standing there when you kissed me?" Max asked her, his eyes narrowed dangerously, and his hands curled into tight balls at his side.

"Max, your wife is insane!" Kendal told him. "You saw how she took off here. I hope she doesn't run someone down in the street." She shook her head. "You're better off without her."

"I'm going to ask you one more time," Max said through gritted teeth, ignoring Kendal's snide remarks about Steph, afraid that if he didn't, he may snap and do something stupid. "Did you know Steph was standing by the gate?"

"I—" Kendal's eyes met his, and hers widened in shock when she saw the anger radiating from his. "I." She licked her lips nervously. "I might have. I can't remember. I was lost in the moment."

"Don't bother going to work tomorrow," Max's voice dipped and dripped with controlled anger. "As of right now, you no longer work there. I'll give you a good reference. There's a job opening in California. I've given the center your details."

"You *can't* fire me!" Kendal's jaw dropped as she stared at him, stunned. "My father will pull his funding from the center."

"I'm sure your father would love to know that you're harassing my wife *again*!" It was no idle threat. Max fully intended to contact Bruno James when he returned to the pool house.

"I haven't been near her!" Kendal retorted. "Besides, she's the crazy one who accused me of harassing her because she was jealous of us."

"There is *no* us and never has been!" Max's anger was rising.

"Oh, come on, Max, you and I both know there's been something between us since the day we met," Kendal insisted. "I knew it the instant you got out of your car and walked toward me."

"My sister-in-law would give me all kinds of grief for hearing me say this," Max told her. "But you're crazy if you think that. There is only one woman in my life. There always has been only Steph and will always be only her!"

"She doesn't deserve you!" Kendal's voice rose as her eyes took on a glassy sheen. "I know you care for me because you've saved me twice!"

"I merely stopped to help someone in distress when I helped with your tire." Max's jaw clamped as a nerve ticked at the side of his jaw. "I didn't know you were inside that burning house." He swallowed, remembering the fire that had ended his career.

"You heard me scream," Kendal pointed out. "I knew you'd come if you heard me scream."

Her voice and the way she was looking at him startled Max. It was as if she wasn't hearing what he was saying but rather what she wanted to hear. Max pulled his phone from his pocket, fearing that this wouldn't end well. When Wallis told Max what Kendal had done to Steph, he wondered if Kendal suffered from mental issues. Right now, he was pretty sure she did.

"I didn't know it was you, Kendal," Max stressed. "All I heard was something screaming in fear."

"No, you heard me, Max. I know you did." Kendal's eyes were glazed. She tilted her head as her eyes fell on the burn scar that ran up his arm. "I didn't mean for you to get hurt. I would never hurt you." Her eyes met his, and his heart stopped for a beat.

What does she mean by that? Max stared at her, fearing he knew what she was about to say next. He quickly hit record on his Dictaphone app to protect himself from anything she might say or do.

"What do you mean I wasn't meant to get hurt in that fire, Kendal?" Max asked her, giving her a wary sideways glance.

"I didn't think it would rage out of control like it did," Kendal confessed. "It was just supposed to be a small fire, but it caught on the curtains and spread so quickly." She stared past him blankly. "Mrs. Berkley was my nanny, and I threatened her to get her out of her house because I knew you'd be running past it." She didn't blink. "Once she was out of the house, I poured gasoline on a small portion of her bedroom and lit it, knowing you'd be running past soon."

"You did what?" Max gasped in disbelief, his ears starting to roar as a mix of emotions flooded him.

"My father imprisoned me in a mental health institution for months after that!" Kendal's eyes became lucid once again and sparked with anger. "This was all *her* fault."

"Who's fault?" Max breathed, fearing he already knew the answer.

"Stephanie's!" Kendal's eyes locked with his. Alarm shot through him at the pure hate he saw shining in them. "She's the one to blame for *everything*. She should've listened to me and just let us be."

"Kendal!" A man's voice echoed toward them, and he barked, "That's enough."

Max turned to see Wallis, two police officers, and Bruno James hurrying toward them.

"Father!" Kendal's face paled as she saw the man striding toward her. "I didn't do anything. I swear."

"I told you to keep away from Max and his family," Bruno growled. "That was the deal and reason I let you work at the Marine Center."

"But I have been, Father, I swear." Kendal sounded like a little girl who'd been caught doing something naughty.

"Wallis?" Max blinked at his friend. "How did you—"

"Dave called to tell me what was happening," Wallis informed Max. "I called the police and Bruno."

"Kendal started that fire on purpose!" Max couldn't believe what he'd heard. "I don't understand why she'd do something like that. I never once led her on." His brow creased as his mind raced, and nothing seemed to make sense. "It wasn't even her house."

"Are you okay, Max?" Scott, the police captain, asked him before frowning. "Did you say Kendal started that fire two years ago deliberately?"

"I don't think that's what you heard, officer!" Bruno stepped in and said warningly to the man.

"Yes, *she* did!" Max was snapped back to reality when he saw Bruno trying to wield his influence over the law. "Scott, I'm sending you the recording of Kendal confessing everything."

"You recorded it?" Scott looked at Max, impressed.

"Yes, I saw Kendal become unstable, and I wanted a record of the conversation in case it went sideways," Max told him.

"You will destroy that recording!" Bruno demanded. "The woman who owned the house didn't press charges, and I made sure it was rebuilt and she was well compensated."

"You bought her silence?" Wallis's brows lifted as he stared at Bruno. "You do realize you've just admitted to that in front of the police captain, an attorney, and a witness."

"Two witnesses," Dave told them from the gate.

"Look, I'll get my daughter back into the facility and make sure she never bothers any of you again," Bruno tried to bargain with them. "I can't have this slur on my name right before the election."

"That's too bad," Scot said, then looked at Max. "Would you come down to the station when you come and give a statement." He held up his phone as it pinged after Max sent the recording to him. "I'll sort the James's out."

"Thanks, Scott," Max said, still feeling like he was dreaming.

He'd nearly died trying to save a woman who'd deliberately set a fire to try and get his attention romantically.

"I'll take Kendal to the police station," Bruno offered.

"I'm sorry, Mr. James, but she has to come with me," Scott told him and called the officer who was with him to take Kendal, who hadn't said a word, away.

"Wow, that's so messed up!" Wallis gave a low whistle.

"Max, before I go," Scott took a step closer and lowered his voice so only Wallis and Max could hear him. "Tom Barnes called me when he couldn't get hold of you or any of the Scott family."

"What did he want?" The name instantly pulled Max's mind out of the funk it was slipping into.

"He found Steph wandering around the shopping mall in a daze," Scott told him. "Tom is with her as she refuses to be taken home and wants Nicky to fetch her."

"Oh, no!" Max closed his eyes and pinched the bridge of his nose. "How could I have pushed what she witnessed to the back of my mind like that?"

He felt like a complete heel. Max had been so stunned by Kendal's revelation that everything else had slipped out of his mind.

"What are you talking about?" Wallis looked at him questioningly.

"I have to go," Scott told them. "If you need any help, let me know."

"Thanks, Scott," Max said, waving the man off. He turned to Wallis. "Can we take your car to get Steph?"

Max started to make his way to Wallis's car, but Wallis stopped him.

"No!" Wallis's voice brooked no argument. "You and I are going to Nicky and explain what has happened. Then you'll come home with me while Nicky gets Steph. When Steph is ready to talk to you, then I'll take you to see her."

"I need to get to my wife!" Max snarled. "Don't try to get in my way."

"Stop it!" Wallis commanded. "You want to hit me, then go ahead. But I'm not letting you go after Steph in this state. I'm trying to help you save your marriage, not end it."

Max took a breath to steady his nerves and shut his eyes, trying to stamp out his anger. Images of the look on Steph's face when she saw Kendal kiss him and her words ripped through him like someone was searing his flesh with a red-hot poker. While all he wanted to do was rush after her and make her listen to him, Max knew Wallis was right.

He slowly opened his eyes and nodded at his friend. "I'm sorry, Wallis." He sighed. "This Kendal business has me all over the place." He clenched his jaw before continuing. "The woman has tried to tear my life apart."

"And if you go barging after Steph now, she'll have succeeded," Wallis pointed out. "Please, buddy, let's do this my way."

"I agree," Max said as he followed Wallis to the car.

Twenty minutes later, Max and Wallis faced a shocked Nicky and Mike in the bookstore as they gave them the footnote version of what had happened.

"Let me get this straight!" Nicky gestured with her hands. "Yours and Steph's marriage has been shaky for two years, and none of us noticed?"

"Nicky, my love," Mike put his arm lovingly around her. "I don't think that's the point right now."

"Oh, I know!" Nicky looked at him, nodding before turning back to Max. "My sister was being stalked and harassed by an unhinged woman obsessed with *you*!"

"I don't think Hannah would approve of your using the term unhinged, sweetheart," Mike pointed out.

"I don't care!" Nicky shrugged. "My younger sister was in danger, and I didn't have a clue about it." Her eyes narrowed angrily at Max. "And neither did you because you were moping about escaping death and your career being ended by that fire."

"Nicky, that's not fair," Wallis, who had never been afraid of Nicky's wrath, stood up for Max.

"Do you want to know what's really unfair?" Nicky's voice rose with her temper. "My sister suffered in silence while still supporting *your friend here*!" She sneered, pointing at Max. "She went through hell putting on a brave face while trying to keep her family together and protected."

"Nicky!" Wallis's voice boomed through the room. "That's enough."

"No, Wallis," Max intervened. "Nicky's right."

"Of course I am." Nicky looked at Wallis smugly before turning her attention back to Max. "You're lucky I like you and have known you for so long, Max." She pursed her lips. "I know you and know you never meant for any of this to happen. You're a good guy, Max. But in the future, think twice about who you stop to help alongside the road."

"I agree with you about everything you've just said," Wallis told her. "But someone needs to get Steph and talk to her." He glanced at Max. "It can't be Max if we want to save their marriage."

"You're right," Nicky conceded. "I'll get Steph and talk to her." She looked at Wallis. "You and Max should go to your house, Wallis. I will call you with an update as soon as I can."

"I'll join you guys," Mike included himself in the plans. "We can get a pizza, as I'm starving, and have a beer while Max calms down and gets his head straight."

"I can liaise with Captain Scott to find out what's going to happen to Kendal," Wallis told them.

As Max, Wallis, and Mike prepared to leave, Max took a moment to speak privately with Nicky. His voice trembled with emotion as he shared his deepest feelings.

"Please tell Steph I love her, and I'm so sorry," Max pleaded. The intensity of his love and regret etched on his face.

Nicky met his gaze, her eyes softening with empathy. "I will," she assured him. "But Max, you must know that while I love you like a brother, Steph *is* my sister, and I'll always put her needs and happiness first."

Max nodded in understanding, his heart aching as he turned to walk away, joining his friends and feeling the weight of the journey ahead. The future with the love of his life hung in the balance, and every step he took toward Wallis's car seemed to feel like he was plunging deeper into the abyss of uncertainty.

CHAPTER 9

Steph sat across the table from Tom, where she'd just once again poured her heart out to the man. He must think she was a complete mess. Steph glanced around the restaurant, remembering she'd been there a few days ago with Hannah—the day she found out she was... Steph shook her head to clear away thoughts of her pregnancy. She had other issues to deal with at the moment. Issues that had left her broken and bleeding on the inside with a wound no modern medicine could heal.

"Steph." Tom's gentle voice drew her attention back to him. "Please don't think I'm taking sides, as I'm here for you. But maybe what you saw wasn't what you thought it was."

At the back of her mind, Steph knew she was being irrational as a surge of anger at Tom's words spread through her veins, and her eyes narrowed. "Are you saying I was seeing things?"

"No!" Tom tilted and turned his head slightly as he shook his head. "I'm saying that by the way, you explained the events leading to the kiss between Tom and ..." He frowned. "What was her name?"

"Kendal!" Steph's voice dripped with bitterness.

"Right, Kendal." Tom nodded. "You did say she smirked smugly at you before leaning in and initiating the kiss."

"I said: Kendal's lips turned into a smirky, smug smile, then she leaned in and kissed Max," Steph corrected him. "Trust me, I *know* what I saw. What I *didn't* see was Max complaining or seeming to mind it!"

"Steph," Tom reached over the table and took her hand. "I'm not trying to anger you, and trust me, from what you've told me, I think Max has issues, but you need to give him a chance to explain."

"Explain!" Steph ripped her hand away from Tom's as the words ripped out her throat, leaving a stinging burn behind them. "He accused *me* of having an affair with you without letting me explain what happened."

"And did you explain what happened to Max?" Tom's question hit a nerve.

"No!" Steph shook her head. "I didn't get a chance to."

"Did you try?" Tom persisted.

"I left to go to my sisters before we could speak," Steph admitted.

"Don't you think the two of you need to talk about what happened with us and with Max and Kendal?" Tom asked her gently.

"I'm not sure it will make a difference now." Steph's gaze moved past Tom and out the window to the busy streets below.

"You don't know that," Tom said encouragingly. "You need to keep your mind open to the possibility that maybe what you saw didn't mean what you think it did." He gave her a tight smile. "Just like what Max saw when you fell and I caught you."

Tom's reasoning started to seep through the anger, betrayal, and pain she was feeling. While her mind agreed with him, her heart and soul retreated behind the sorrow.

"Steph!" Nicky's voice rang from behind her.

Steph turned to see her older sister rushing toward her.

"Nicky?" Steph frowned as Nicky stopped at their table.

"Hi," Nicky said, giving a small wave and looking toward Tom. "Hi, Tom."

"Hey, Nicky," Tom greeted her back.

"I see you and Tom have already met," Steph commented.

"Yes, Tom's one of Mike's good friends," Nicky explained, pulling up a chair and sitting.

"Of course." Steph nodded, remembering Nicky's mention that Mike, her fiance, knew Tom and his father. "What are you doing here?"

"I came to get you," Nicky told her and glanced at Tom. "Tom called me to let me know you were here, and when he found you, you were upset."

"Traitor!" Steph looked at Tom accusingly.

"Sorry, Steph, I was worried about you," Tom flashed Nicky a disapproving look before smiling warmly at Steph. "But that's *all* I told her."

"Thank you." Steph smiled gratefully at him, knowing what he meant.

"Why don't you come back to the cottage with me for the night?" Nicky invited Steph. "We can have a girl's night in, and you can spend some time with your baby niece."

The mention of babies set Steph's pulse racing once again, and anxiety joined the party of emotions already wreaking havoc on her nervous system.

"I'd prefer just to go home," Steph told her, then looked at Tom. "Would you mind giving me a lift if you're going back to the hotel?"

"I'll give you a lift," Nicky offered. "Thank you, Tom, for looking out for Steph, but I'll get her home."

"Of course," Tom said with a nod and looked for clarification for Steph. "Are you okay with that, Steph?" He raised his eyebrows. "Because I don't mind taking you home if you want me to."

"No, it's fine, I'll go with Nicky," Steph told him. "You've been so kind, and I've taken up so much of your time today already."

"I'm always a phone call away if you need me," Tom assured her.

Tom settled the bill, and the three of them left the restaurant. Tom walked them to Nicky's car and ensured Steph was okay before leaving. Steph and Nicky left the mall parking, heading back to Scott House as a thought struck Steph.

"Tom is a really nice guy," Steph turned toward Nicky.

"Yes, he is," Nicky agreed.

"I think he and Lorry would make a good pair." Steph grinned at the look Nicky shot her.

"Tom is one of the nicest men I've met in a long time," Nicky stated. "But Steph, please don't go trying out your matchmaking skill on Lorry again. The last time was a disaster."

Thinking of their eldest sister and Steph's last attempt to matchmake her made Steph smile. Nicky was right in saying it had been a disaster, but only because Lorry knew she was being set up and immediately did the Lorry thing where she went on the defensive.

"Granted, that attempt had failed miserably," Steph agreed with Nicky. "But I've learned from that mistake, and this time, Lorry won't realize she's being set up until it's too late." She bit her lip thoughtfully. "Lorry and Tom are already working together. It wouldn't take much."

"That's thoughtful of you to think of Lorry's happiness and want someone as nice as Tom for her." Nicky glanced at Steph. "But little sister, don't you think you should fix your own love life before trying to fiddle with other people's?"

Alarm shot through Steph when she realized that Nicky must know about her and Max's strained relationship.

"Did Tom tell you?" Steph didn't believe he would do that, but she had to ask.

"No, I haven't spoken to Tom the whole day," Nicky told her before she realized what she'd said.

"But I thought he called you about me," Steph caught Nicky out in her lie.

"Okay!" Nicky breathed, turning into Tigertail Avenue, where Scott House, The Scott Hotel, Steph's house, Nicky's cottage, and the bookstore were located. "Tom wasn't the one who told me you needed help." She kept her attention on the road. "Tom did try to call me first, but when I didn't answer, he called Captain Andy."

"Tom called the police?" Steph looked at Nicky in disbelief.

"Yes." Nicky nodded. "Captain Andy and Wallis told Max who came to me."

"I feel a little giddy keeping up with the chain of origin from that story," Steph said sarcastically. Her heart had skipped a painful beat at the mention of Max. "Why didn't Max come to get me?"

"Because Wallis advised him not to," Nicky answered. "They came to me instead." She glanced at Steph once again. "Steph, Max told me *everything*."

"Including that, he accused me of having an affair with Tom?" Steph folded her arms defiantly across her. *Nicky always took Max's side.* "You always take Max's side."

"No, I do *not*!" Nicky growled, hurt flashing in her eyes. "If you must know, I pointed out what an idiot Max had been, and while I loved him like a brother, you're my sister. Your happiness and needs will always come first with me."

"You told him that?" Steph looked at Nicky, impressed.

"Of course I did," Nicky assured her. "And I meant every word of it." She glanced at Steph before pulling into Scott House's driveway.

"Are you sure you don't want to come home with me to my new little cottage?"

"No." Steph shook her head. "You're right. It's time for Max and I to have our showdown."

"You sound like the start of a cowboy movie." Nicky laughed. "Do you want me to come inside with you?"

Steph glanced at the house and noticed that their mother's car wasn't in the drive and their grandmother's bedroom window was closed.

"No, I'll be fine." Steph opened the car door. "It looks like Mom and Gran are out."

"Yes, they've gone to Mom's friend, Marie, for a few days," Nicky told her.

"I don't want this to sound terrible, but that's such a relief to know." Steph blew out a breath. "I really just need a few moments of alone time before facing Max."

Her eyes widened as she realized Max may be at home in the pool house.

Realizing what Steph had, Nicky reassured her, "Don't worry, Max went to stay at Wallis's house until I tell him you want to talk."

"Thanks, Nicky." Steph breathed a sigh of relief. "Please don't tell any of our other family members about all this."

"I won't," Nicky promised, watching Steph climb out of the car. "Where's your car?"

"Max has it," Step explained about the rental she'd dropped off when Tom had found her. "Oh shoot!" She snapped her fingers. "Tom has my bags."

"Don't worry, I'll get them from him," Nicky offered.

"I'd appreciate that." Steph gave her sister a tight smile. "I want to go and take a long soak in the bath and a nap before deciding what to do about—" She had to catch herself before blurting out that she was pregnant. "Things."

"Let me know what you want me to tell Max," Nicky leaned down to look at Steph standing by the car door.

"Tell him to come round to the pool house at seven tonight," Steph instructed.

She said goodbye to Nicky and warily made her way to the pool house. Steph was about to let herself in when a shadow loomed behind her, reflecting in the glass door. Her eyes widened as she saw an object about to be brought down on her head. Steph's first thought went to the life growing inside her, and her eyes pinned on the image of the boulder about to be brought down on her head. She knew if it did, it would most likely kill her. Steph's hands flew protectively to her bells as the mirror image in the glass door moved toward her skull, and she managed to step aside before it hit her.

The boulder-looking object hit the glass door with a resounding crash that echoed with the splintering sound of glass breaking. Steph turned aside, her hands tightening over her belly to protect it from the glass that flew everywhere from the boulder's impact. As the noise died down, Steph's fight or flight instinct kicked in, and she was about to run when long fingers with talon-like nails gripped her arm and dug into Steph's soft flesh.

"Where do you think you're going?" the familiar voice slurred angrily.

Her own temper flared as she realized who had tried to kill her. Red, hazy dots of rage blurred her vision as the flight instinct was overruled by her fight one. Steph, not caring where the punch landed, turned toward her attacker swinging. Pain crunched through her knuckles as she connected with the hard jaw of her surprised assailant. Steph was sure she'd broken her hand. She'd wallop the person so hard. While she wasn't a violent person, nor did she condone violence, Steph felt a wave of satisfaction at having defended herself. Her would-be attacker staggered backward, wide-eyed with disbelief.

"Steph!" Max's voice distracted as the person regained their ground and rushed at Steph. "Stop!"

Before Steph was tackled to the ground, she dodged the attack and shoved the person into the pool.

"Steph, my word!" Nicky rushed toward her.

Nicky engulfed Steph in her arms as Max joined in the hug, not caring what Steph's reaction would be, and for the moment, she let him join in, enjoying the feeling of comfort. The adrenaline was dying, and the reality of what happened began to sink in. Before Steph could stop it, she burst into tears.

"Oh, no, Steph!" Nicky's voice was gravely with emotion as her eyes misted over. "Honey, it's over now. You're safe."

"Steph, I'm so sorry," Max's voice was soft as he pulled away from the woman and stepped aside to let Nicky take her inside.

He was about to follow them inside when Wallis called to them. The three of them turned to see Captain Andy, a few of his officers, and Wallis retrieving Kendal James from the swimming pool.

"I thought you said she was in jail or an asylum?" Nicky hissed at Max.

"So did we until Andy called to tell us that Kendal had escaped, and he was sure she was looking for Steph," Max explained. "We called Tom, who told us you'd taken Steph home, and we came straight here."

They watched a spitting, mad, wet Kendal, enraged and trying to push the police officers off her.

"Let me go!" Kendal screamed at them.

But the female officer managed to restrain and cuff Kendal.

"Wow!" Nicky's eyes widened, and she shook her head before turning her attention back to Steph, who was wiping her eyes and regaining control over her hyper-sensitive emotions. "Are you okay?" Her eyes examined Steph. "Did she hurt you?"

"Only my hand!" Steph held up her swollen, throbbing hand. "I may have punched her when she was trying to detain me."

"Steph!" Nicky and Max said in unison as they stared at soft and gentle Steph's hand.

"She was trying to hurt my—" Steph stopped herself and corrected, "Trying to hurt me."

"We're not judging!" Nicky held up her hands.

"Let me see that," Max said, gently taking her hand to examine it. "You need X-rays, Steph."

He looked at her, and their eyes locked.

"I'm sure it's just bruised," Steph stared into his warm eyes, and the tears started to well up once again. *Darn, these over-sensitive hormones of mine.* She gave herself a mental shake.

"Nicky!" Mike's voice caught Nicky's attention as he ran toward them. "Are you okay?"

"I'm fine," Nicky assured him and turned to look proudly at Steph. "But my amazing sister here just fended off an attacker."

"Let me take you to the emergency room." Max ignored the people around them, never taking his eyes off Stephs.

Steph didn't trust herself to speak and nodded.

"Excuse us," Max put his arm through Steph, gently holding her injured one. "I'm taking Steph to Naples to get her hand checked out."

"Okay!" Nicky nodded with a small smile. "I'll sort things out here."

"I'll get Tom to fix the door and help clean up the mess," Mike offered.

Steph and Max didn't say a word as they walked to her car, which Max was still driving. It wasn't until they'd left Bar Harbor and were heading toward Naples that either of them spoke.

"Steph, I promise you nothing is going on between myself and Kendal, and there never was." Max glanced at her. "I know I've been difficult to live with since the fire." Steph saw his knuckles whiten on the steering as his grip tightened on it. "I've been a moping selfish fool who didn't want to admit to how deeply nearly dying in that fire affected me."

"You've had a lot to deal with." Steph's voice was soft, and she looked down at her aching hand cradled in her lap.

"I should've let you in so we could've dealt with it together like we've always done," Max admitted.

Steph looked at him. "Why didn't you?"

Max looked at her, his eyes haunted. "Because I feared you'd think less of me."

"Max!" Steph's heart squeezed. "I could never think that of you." A stray tear stagged down her cheek, and she swiped it away with her good hand. "I felt I had somehow let you down that you didn't want to let me in."

"No, Steph!" Max touched her arm and gave it a loving squeeze. "You were my strength all the way." She saw his jaw clench and that he was fighting for control. "Every day I looked that angry, it reminded me of the fire that scarred my body, and I felt so ashamed."

"Why?" Steph's brow furrowed as she looked at him. "Your scars are the testament to what you survived. They remind me how strong you are to have survived what you did and how thankful I am that you're still with us today." She swallowed, her throat burning from suppressed tears that she didn't know how much longer she could hold back. "You have nothing to be ashamed of, Max." She gave him a small smile. "And everything to be proud of and grateful for."

"That's why I love you so much, Steph." Max pulled to the side of the road when he came to a stop-over place. He turned to her and took her hand. "I've never wanted to even look at another woman, Steph. It's only ever been you, and only ever will be you."

"Max—" But she didn't get any further as Max stopped her.

"Please, let me finish," Max said, and Steph nodded. "I'm so sorry about Kendal. I didn't know and was so wrapped up in becoming captain before the fire I didn't realize she was stalking you." His brows knit together. "I didn't even see the signs of how obsessed she was."

"It's not your fault, Max," Steph assured him. "You have a huge heart and are that person who's always willing to give a helping hand." She gave him a watery smile. "How were you to know that Kendal had some sort of obsessive disorder?"

"I'm so sorry!" Max said again. His eyes filled with pain and regret. "I go cold thinking of how she could've hurt you or the twins."

"It's over now," Steph said.

"There's something you should know about the fire," Max told her, explaining how Kendal had deliberately started it.

"That takes her obsession to a whole other level!" Steph stared at Max in shocked disbelief. Her heart squeezed, and anger churned in her for how Kendal had nearly killed Max. "I hate that she put you through all that, all because you did a good deed."

"I'm sorry my good deed nearly got you badly hurt and nearly destroyed our marriage." Max stopped, his face turning serious as he looked at her. "She hasn't completely destroyed it, has she?" He swallowed. "Or did I do that all on my own with my self-pity?"

"Neither." Steph's heart lifted and flooded with love once again as she stared into the eyes of the man that she loved so much. "I should've said something about Kendal when she started causing trouble." She chewed on her bottom lip. "You had so much on your plate with work I didn't want to distract you."

"Why don't we make a pact?" Max suggested.

"I'm listening." Steph's brow furrowed as she watched him.

"From this moment forward, we don't keep anything for the other, no matter the consequence or if we think the other one is too stressed or busy," Max laid out the plan.

"I can agree to that," Steph said, a twinge of guilt slicing through her as she knew it was her turn for confessions and apologies.

"Steph, after all these years together, you have to know I'm still as head over heels in love with you as I was the first day we met." Max leaned forward, and their lips met.

Steph's breath caught in her throat as she savored their closeness. When Max ended the kiss and pulled away, Steph wanted to reach out and pull him back, but she stopped herself.

Now is the best time to get this said, Steph! She gave herself a talking-to. "I love you so much, too, Max." Her eyes locked with his. "You're my soulmate and the only man I ever want to share my life with."

"What would you say to us going to couples therapy?" Max blurted out.

At first, the thought seemed to slap her in the face and offend her, thinking Max thought they needed counseling. But as the initial shock wore off, Steph knew it would be a good idea. They'd been through so much since her father passed away three years ago that therapy could only make them stronger.

"I don't think it would hurt," Steph agreed.

"Great!" Max grinned, and for the first time in a long time, Steph saw it light up his eyes. "Now, let's get your hand sorted out, Mike Tyson," he teased.

"Wait, Max, before we leave, I have something to say," Steph stopped him from driving off.

"Okay," Max said, settling back in the car seat and looking at her questioningly.

"Nothing is going on between Tom and I. I tripped and he caught me," Steph confessed.

"I know," Max said, with a confirmation nod. "Tom told me after you went to Palm Beach with Hannah." He leaned over and kissed her again. "I never should've even for a minute entertained the idea you were cheating on me."

"We were both edgy," Steph said. "But that's not all I need to tell you."

Max frowned as he noticed the look on her face. "What is it, Steph?" He reached over and took her hand reassuringly. "You can tell me whatever it is."

Steph was sure she could see him holding his breath.

"I didn't faint the other day because of that silly diet," Steph murmured.

Max's face fell, and worry sparked in his eyes.

"Why did you faint, then?" Max's voice was rough with emotion, and his eyes darkened.

"I'm eight weeks pregnant!" Steph felt relief wash over her as the words tumbled from her lips.

Max's eyes widened as he stared at her for the next five minutes in stunned silence.

EPILOGUE

Six Months Later

Steph's feet were swollen, and her belly was huge. She was sure she was having twins again, but the doctor assured her only one baby was growing inside her. Steph knew her family, sons, and Max, even though he never let on, all thought she was overly hormonal. But Steph was convinced the doctor was wrong. She'd felt two babies kicking her, and she was sure she'd seen a hand pop up on either side of her belly simultaneously. So unless her baby had a very wide reach, that was two babies.

Because of her last pregnancy, Steph and Max had been paranoid about making sure nothing went wrong. Steph had even refused to have unnecessary ultrasounds, and they didn't want to know if it was a girl or boy this time. Excitement zapped through her as she got ready for Max to take her to Naples for her thirty-two-week ultrasound. Not wanting to have the stress of the trip to Naples for her checkups, Steph had been going to the local clinic on Marco Island. While the staff had been great, they didn't have the ultra-modern ultrasound machines the hospital in Naples had.

Today, Steph and Max would see their baby, or babies, as Steph was convinced it was twins again, in three-D. She heard the knock at the door and knew it was Nicky. She and Mike were going to be watching Liam and Jack. Max and Steph were going to make a romantic weekend out of the trip before their new baby joined their family. She smiled as she slipped on her shoes and made her way downstairs.

These past six months had been a whirlwind of moving into their beautifully renovated house, getting the twins ready for their new sibling, and Max and Steph rebuilding their relationship. Her heart skipped a beat when she saw Max open the door and greet Nicky and Mike. They had been going to couples therapy twice a month, and it had helped them overcome the issues that had started to tear them apart. On top of the couples therapy, Max was going to therapy to address the trauma of the fire.

Life was good once again, and each day, it got better. Steph rubbed her belly, and soon, there would be a new addition to their family. She smiled as she felt the kicks.

"Hey." Steph rubbed the spots. "Stop that. You're going to make Mommy want to go to the toilet again, and you know we're going to Naples today."

While Steph still feared the birth, she was a lot calmer about it, knowing that the doctor who was going to deliver the baby was more prepared this time. Because of her last pregnancy, Steph would have a cesarean this time. And whatever happened, Steph was prepared for it and felt hopeful that everything would be okay.

"Hey, little sister," Nicky's voice snapped Steph from her musings. "You're looking radiant."

"Thank you," Steph grinned, waddling down the stairs. Because that's what she did these days: waddle like a lopsided duck. "But I know you're really thinking—wow, you're huge."

"And really touchy!" Nicky rolled her eyes, hugging Steph when she joined them by the door.

"Are you ready to go, my love?" Max kissed her brow. "We have to leave if we're going to make the doctor's appointment."

Steph and Max said goodbye to their sons, Nicky, and Mike, and were soon on their way to Naples. True to form, while Steph tried to make a concerted effort to stay awake during the trip, she was lights out shortly after they left Marco Island city limits. Steph was woken by Max gently kissing her brow to wake her.

"Hey, Sleeping Beauty." Max smiled as her eyes fluttered open. "We're here."

Steph yawned and stretched as the world came into focus. Max climbed out of the car and rushed around to her side to help her out, or she would have to rock herself from the seat. Steph knew she must look like a tortoise stuck on its back and trying to rock itself onto its feet.

While they were sitting in the waiting room, pain shot through Steph's abdomen. She winced and grabbed her stomach.

"Steph!" Max said in a panic. "What's wrong?"

"Ow!" Steph said through clenched teeth as another pain stabbed her belly. "I don't know." She winced.

Max was out of the chair and flagging down a nurse at record speed.

"My wife had suddenly got a lot of pain in her stomach." Steph could hear the panic in Max's voice.

"I'll check on her, Mr. Victor," the nurse told him, following him to Steph. She knelt before Steph. "Mrs. Victor, can you tell me where the pain is and what kind of pain it is."

"A sharp pain in my lower abdomen," Steph explained.

"Can you walk?" the nurse asked Steph, who nodded.

The nurse and Max helped Steph to her feet as another pain struck, and she doubled over.

"Breathe through the pain, Mrs. Victor," the nurse's voice was calm and gentle.

When the pain subsided, Max and the nurse guided Steph into the examination room of the doctor's surgery, which was located at Naples Medical Center. It was a new state-of-the-art hospital where one of Florida's top OB/GYN, Doctor Phillips.

The nurse helped Steph into an examination gown while Max paced impatiently behind the closed curtains. When Doctor Phillips entered the room, Steph had barely gotten comfortable on the examination bed.

"Hello, Victor family," Doctor Phillips's cheerful voice filled the room, which warmed with his smile. "Nurse Jenkins tells me you're experiencing some pain, Mrs. Victor."

Doctor Phillips pulled on latex gloves as he got ready to examine Steph.

"Oh, just some minor ones," Steph tried to fob it off as she didn't want to let the fear or panic that were trying to break into her positivity in. "It's probably wind."

"I noticed in your records from Marco Island Clinic that you haven't yet had a three-D sonogram," Doctor Phillips commented. "You've had TVUS in your first trimester and two two-D ultrasounds in your second and third trimesters."

"That's right," Max answered, and Steph took his hand. She could feel how nervous he was.

Steph knew, like her, that as soon as the pain had gripped her, his mind had gone back to the day the twins were born. The pain she was experiencing had been similar to the way the pain had started that day.

"Okay, let's take a look, shall we?" Doctor Phillips moved next to Steph and got the machine ready.

The nurse covered part of Steph's body with a sheet, exposing her rounded belly to coat it with gel. Steph's breath caught in her throat as the initial cold hit her, making her baby kick out in protest.

"Goodness, that little one doesn't like the cold." The nurse smiled and stepped away as Doctor Phillips positioned the machine. As soon as he did, the sound of the heartbeat filled their ears.

"Oh my!" Doctor Phillips said, squinting at the screen.

"What is it?" Steph craned her neck to see the screen, and Max leaned over her to get a better look.

Before he could reply, the nurse caught their attention. "Excuse me, Doctor Phillips." She pointed to the bed.

"Oh dear!" Doctor Phillips's brows rose.

"What is it?" Steph and Max chorused, their voices slightly raised in panic.

"I don't know how to tell you this," Doctor Phillips put his hands on the monitor, preparing to turn it toward them. "But the doctor on Marco Island got it wrong." He turned the monitor, making Max and Steph gasp. "You're having twins." He glanced at the wet patch seeping onto the sheets. "And from the look of it, your twins want to meet their parents today."

While Max gaped at the doctor in shock, Steph laughed as she turned to Max, saying smugly, "I *told* you all that I was having twins!"

But her smugness was wiped from her face as pain sliced through her belly again, and her laughter turned to an agonizing groan. The next hour passed by in a blur of hospital walls rushing by, masked medical staff gathered around her. Max was by her side the entire time, gripping her hand and chewing the nails of his free hand. Steph could feel Max's anxiety mirrored her own, and it was like they were both holding their breath until the doctor placed two healthy babies in their arms.

"Victor family, meet your twin daughters," Doctor Phillips smiled as he gently handed Steph the tiny girls. "We'll need to take them to the nursery, but I thought you may want to see them first."

"They're gorgeous," Max's voice was hoarse with emotions, and his eyes were filled with tears. "We have daughters, Steph."

"Yes, I think we should name them Faith and Hope." Steph's own eyes filled with tears, and the nurses took them away.

"I love those names." Max kissed Steph and followed beside her as she was wheeled to the recovery room.

Steph's heart was once again whole filled with the accomplishment of bringing new life into the world and she knew that whatever lay ahead, they'd be able to face it together as they once again navigated the beautiful chaos of parenthood.

*It would mean a lot to me if you would be so kind as to leave me an honest review for **The Baby on Marco Island**. As an independent author, it helps me reach more readers, and we help readers discover books they like.*

A very short review would be more than enough. It only has to be a line or two. Please do not feel it has to be a long paragraph.

The link I have placed below makes it so easy. It is a special link that takes you straight to the review section. Thank you in advance, and I appreciate you.

Amy and Rose

Amazon.com/review/create-review?&asin=B0CKFPBF5P

CONTINUE READING

SCOTT SISTERS SERIES - BOOK 3

THE BACHELOR ON MARCO ISLAND

CHAPTER 1

The early morning sun painted Tigertail Avenue in soft pastel hues as Lorry Scott stepped onto the balcony of her apartment on the top floor of the Scott family's historic hotel. Her temples throbbed in rhythm with the distant sounds of construction that already reverberated through the air. The day had barely begun, and the pounding in her head was aggravated by the relentless clamor of renovations that, by agreement, weren't supposed to commence until after nine in the morning.

As one of the hotel's owners, her responsibilities had multiplied in recent months, thanks to the ongoing renovations and the unexpected challenges that life had thrown her way. Her sister, Steph, who helped her run and manage the hotel, was now on maternity leave after the arrival of twin baby girls, Faith and Hope. Steph's absence left Lorry shouldering the burden alone, navigating the intricacies of the day-to-day operations and heavy duties of hotel management. The weight of overseeing renovations—a task she had been opposed to from the start—pressed heavily on her shoulders.

Lorry looked out over the sea. The once serene island had become a canvas for change, a transformation that she was reluctant to embrace, especially now that their charming hotel with a rich history stood in the midst of renovation chaos. Lorry couldn't even enjoy her usual few moments of peace and fresh air she took before she went to work. The fresh early morning sea air hung heavy with the stench of pain while the serene sound of the waves gently lapping the shore was drowned out by the sounds of construction echoing through the air. The noise didn't help the tension that Lorry had developed from her fight with her angry teenage daughter, Tammy, over visiting her father for the summer.

Lately, with each passing day, it felt as if the threads holding the fabric of Lorry's life together were fraying. The argument with Tammy, who was growing more rebellious by the day, lingered in the air like an unresolved chord adding to the hotel's chaos. Her eyes fell on a tall, well-built man with sandy brown hair entering the hotel, and her irritation grew—Tom Barnes, the architect of the upheaval in her hotel. Tom's father, James, owned Barnes Construction, the contractors working on the renovations with Tom at the helm.

Lorry had a strong inkling that her mother Pat, who had instigated the renovations and hired the construction company to do them, was romantically involved with James. The thought of her mother dating another man sent a wave of anger through her. She knew it was unjust and childish, as her father had passed away three years ago, but it still felt like Lorry's mother was betraying him. To Lorry, it was another reason to dislike the Barnes men and make her set against the renovations. Renovations that had encountered nothing but unexpected delays since they'd begun nearly a year ago.

Lorry took another deep breath and rubbed her throbbing temples. With a heavy heart and her world seemingly on the brink of unraveling, she walked back into the living room. Tammy had left to go surfing with her cousins, Liam and Jack. While she loved her daughter more than anything in the world, a bit of tension left Lorry as the silence of the apartment embraced her. That was until she turned into the kitchen and found Tammy's clothes scattered like bread crumbs as she'd undressed down the hallway.

Her head fell back onto her shoulders as Lorry stared up at the ceiling and breathed before shaking her head and picking up the discarded garments. She decided not to go into Tammy's room as she could imagine the state of it. Tammy loved to wreck her room when she was angry with Lorry.

"I don't have the strength for that room right now," Lorry mumbled, turning into the family bathroom and dumping Tammy's clothes into a laundry bin.

As she shoved a pair of shorts that fell back out of the bin, a photo fell out of one of the pockets. Lorry bent and scooped it up, her heart freezing when she read the back of it.

This is my new daughter - Glory.

Lorry turned the picture over. A spurt of anger shot through her at the face of her ex-husband, Grant, and his new wife, Jackie, with their newborn baby. She had to stop herself from ripping it up. Not because she was jealous of Grant or his new family. Lorry had been over Grant a few years before the divorce ten years ago. The anger she felt toward him was because of Tammy. He was the most insensitive father.

Lorry's phone rang, distracting her. She shoved the photo into the pocket of her high-waisted maroon cotton slacks that hugged her flat belly with two rows of gold buttons before the wide bottoms floated just above the floor. Lorry answered the phone while turning to the bathroom mirror and straightening her cream cotton blouse with an off-center V-neck and short sleeves.

"Lorry Scott," Lorry said into the phone, smoothing out the soft, messy bun her shoulder length soft, thick, strawberry blonde hair was pulled into.

"Hi, sweetheart," Pat Scott's voice echoed through the receiver.

"Mom?" Lorry's brows furrowed as she checked the number on the phone. It was listed as an unknown number. "What number is this?"

"I borrowed a friend of mine's phone at the country club," Pat explained.

"Where's your phone?" Lorry asked, worry creeping in to top off all the other stressful emotions that had started her day.

"That's why I'm calling," Pat told her with a catch in her voice that, over the years, Lorry knew well—her mother needed help. "I've had a little mishap."

"Oh no!" Lorry's eyes widened as she exited the bathroom and hurried back down the hallway, grabbing her car keys from the bowl on the table next to the front door.

"Are you grabbing your car keys?" Pat asked.

"Yes, I'm on my way," Lorry said.

"I haven't even told you what's happened!" Pat exclaimed.

"Mom, I've known you for forty-eight years." Lorry slung her purse over her shoulder and yanked open the front door. "I know that tone in your voice. You need my help."

"You always were the most perceptive out of my daughters." Pat sighed.

"I think that would be Hannah," Lorry corrected as she rushed to the private elevator and pressed the button to call it.

"There's no hurry, sweetheart," Pat assured her.

"I'm already on my way," Lorry told her, glancing at her wristwatch, her frown returning. "Why are you at the country club so early?"

"I'm helping Marjorie set up for her daughter's wedding," Pat answered.

"On a Friday?" Lorry pushed the elevator button several times, wondering why it was taking so long. "What the heck is wrong with the elevator?"

"Did you fight with Tammy?" Pat's question made Lorry grit her teeth and shake her head.

"Right!" Lorry hissed, turning and walking toward the stairs. "I'm going to take the elevator keys away from her."

"You won't have to worry about her locking it from downstairs once the new system has been installed," Pat told her.

"Do you want me to come help you?" Lorry asked warningly. "Because reminding me of all the disruption and new-aged systems being installed at the hotel is not endearing me to want to help you."

"Sweetheart," Pat was about to say more, but Lorry stopped her.

"Let's not get into this again, Mom, please," Lorry started down the stairs. "Why don't you tell me what's happened that you've had to phone me on your friend's phone instead?"

"You sound stressed!" Pat hedged. "I don't know if I want to add to that." She paused. "Maybe I should call Nicky."

"Mom!" Lorry was already passing the hotel's second floor. "You're adding to my stress by hedging." Her voice raised slightly. "Now tell me, what's going on?"

"As it was a nice day, I decided to walk to the club," Pat began her story.

"Walk?" Lorry asked in disbelief. "Mom, the club is on the opposite side of the island to us. Why on earth would you walk there?"

"I wasn't at home," Pat informed her, setting off alarm bells in Lorry's head. "I was having an early breakfast with a friend who lives at the golf estate, which, as you know, is a block away from the club."

"Who is this friend?" Lorry didn't have to ask as she knew it was James Barnes.

"Who my friend is isn't the issue here," Pat said in a prickly voice, which meant she wasn't going to tell Lorry. "On the way, some kid swooped past me on a bicycle and snatched my purse, which had my car keys, wallet, house keys, phone, and make-up in it."

"Mom!" Lorry gasped, stopping as she was about to open the ground-floor stairwell door. Her heart had started to hammer in fright at the thought of her mother being mugged. "Are you okay?"

"I'm shaken, and I had a bit of a fall from my purse being yanked so hard off my arm," Pat told her. "But other than a few scrapes, bruises, and losing my items, I'm fine."

"I'm on my way," Lorry told her, shoving the door open only to have it hit an obstruction. "What the—"

"Hey!" A startled male voice yelped from the other side.

Before Lorry could take her hand off the door handle, the door was yanked open, pulling her with it. Her phone and purse went flying alongside Lorry, who landed up thudding into Tom Barnes.

"You!" Lorry sneered, fumbling to push herself from his wall of muscled chest.

"You!" Tom growled at the same time.

They stood looking at each other with narrowed eyes and crumpled brows until Pat's worried cries resounded from Lorry's phone on the floor.

"Lorry?" Pat called. "Sweetheart, what's going on?" Her voice raised a little higher. "Lorry!"

Lorry bent down to get her phone at the same time Tom did, and their heads collided.

"Good grief!" Lorry's voice rang with annoyance as she held her forehead, not needing the extra pain searing through it.

"You saw I was going to pick it up!" Tom scooped up her phone and handed it to her. "Are you okay?"

"No thanks to you!" Lorry snatched her phone from his hand before sidestepping the mountain of muscle. "I'm going to pick up my purse now."

She glanced at him and pointed to the floor where it lay.

"I wasn't going to attempt to touch another of your items." Tom gave her a tight smile before turning and walking off.

"That arrogant jerk!" Lorry grabbed her purse from the ground and quickly scanned the area where it fell to ensure nothing had fallen out of it before heading for the parking garage.

"Who's an arrogant jerk?"

Lorry was so irritated by her encounter with Tom she'd almost forgotten her mother was still on the line.

"No one," Lorry said, not wanting to start a debate with her mother, who adored the Barnes men. "I'm going to hang up now as I'm nearly at my car. I'll be at the club in ten to fifteen minutes." She stopped as she walked into the parking garage and sighed. "Shoot. Mom, I have to go. I'd better let Hailey know where I am."

"Okay, sweetheart." Pat said goodbye, and they hung up.

Lorry quickly returned to the hotel's foyer, carefully making sure Tom was nowhere in sight as she made a dash for the front desk. Hailey Ingram was the hotel's concierge, managing the staff while Steph was away. Ross Berkley, currently handling the front desk, was one of their newer hires. He'd been with them for just over a year.

"Hi, Ross," Lorry greeted him.

"Good morning, Lorry," Ross greeted her back with his usual friendly smile and far too chirpy for that time of day attitude.

"Will you please let Hailey and anyone else who may be looking for me know that I have to run an important errand." Lorry looked at her wristwatch. "I shouldn't be longer than two hours at the most."

"Of course," Ross said.

Lorry hurried back toward the parking garage. As she got near the door, she heard the familiar sound her phone made when she got a personal email. She opened up the mail and smiled. It was her pen pal—TJ Bean.

I hope you have a better day than yesterday. Mine started out great when I opened my email to find one from you.

TJ xx

They'd been writing to each other since just after her father died. Lorry had been going through her father's personal email account when she found a new email from someone named TJ Bean. It was the most heartfelt email she'd ever read. At first, Lorry had been so stunned, and her worst fears about her father having had an affair appeared to be true. The letter was addressed to Robby, a nickname Lorry's grandmother and sometimes mother had called her father.

While she'd read the letter, Lorry's shock and disbelief had melted into tears as she'd read the love letter. When she came to the end of the letter, she realized it wasn't for her father and must've been sent to the wrong email as it was signed: You'll always be my first love, my one big love, and the mother of our daughter - your ex-husband T. J. Bean.

With a mixture of guilt and something else driving her, Lorry had written to T. J., letting him know he'd sent the email to the wrong address. The next day, Lorry had been surprised to find he'd written back, and they'd struck up a friendship. His ex-wife's name was Robby Scot, and TJ's ex-wife's email was RScot, while Lorry's father was RScott. All it took was one missing letter to bring two people together.

Well, two pen pals together anyway. They had never met in person, talked, or messaged over the phone. Lorry didn't know TJ's phone number or his full name, and he didn't know those details about her either. He thought she was Robby Scott. They'd been emailing each other more than once every day for the past three years since she'd responded to his wrongly sent letter. While they didn't know those details about each other, they knew much deeper things about each other.

"Lorry!" Tom's voice snapped her out of her reverie before she could read TJ's letter.

"What?" Lorry snapped, looking up and realizing she was standing next to his pickup truck in the place her car should've been. "Where's my car?"

She glanced around the garage.

"You loaned it to Nicky last night," Tom reminded her.

"But I have the…" Lorry held the keys in her hand and realized they were spare keys for the hotel shuttle bus. She looked at where that was usually parked, and it was out. "Shoot!"

"What's the matter?" Tom asked her.

"I have to fetch my mother from the country club," Lorry muttered, about to phone Steph and find out if she could borrow her car.

"I can give you a lift," Tom offered. "My pickup is a double cab."

Lorry was about to decline his offer, but it would save time.

"Sure, if it's not too much trouble," Lorry accepted his offer.

"Not at all," Tom assured her, pulling open the passenger door. "I was headed out to pick up refreshments for my crew."

Lorry nodded and climbed into the vehicle.

"I'm sorry the crew started ahead of schedule this morning," Tom surprised Lorry by saying as he pulled out of the garage and headed toward the club. "They were behind due to the rain these past two days and wanted to make up the work."

"That's fine," Lorry said curtly. A pang of guilt seeped through her about the way she'd replied, as Tom was being friendly by going to pick up her mother and not letting an awkward silence fall between them. "I appreciate their enthusiasm, but we do have guests to consider."

"I can assure you Barry, the foreman, went door to door last night to inform the guests that they would be starting early," Tom told her. "They'll be working late today as well."

"That should be fine." Lorry nodded.

She was proud of herself for biting her tongue and not letting Tom know how she felt about the contractors starting early and working late. While Lorry would give anything to be able to kick them out, the quicker they got the work done, the faster they'd be out of the hotel, taking their bosses with them.

Tom spoke about upgrading the swimming pool for the rest of the journey. A project that Lorry had initiated and was what had prompted her mother to start a full upgrade of the hotel. The swimming pool was last upgraded when Lorry was eight which was a long time ago. It had only taken nearly a year for Barnes Contractors to finally start on the pool. Lorry pushed that thought from her mind reminding herself that Tom was being kind and getting irritated with him would be rude. Thankfully, the journey didn't take long, and soon they were pulling into the parking area of the country club. Lorry was barely out of the pickup when her mother rushed out the front door.

"You won't believe what's happened." Pat was out of breath as she rushed toward Lorry and Tom, holding her purse in her hands. "A jogger saw what happened and chased the person who mugged me."

"Really?" Lorry's brows shot up in amazement.

"You were mugged?" Tom's face fell as he gazed at Pat in disbelief before looking accusingly at Lorry. "You never mentioned your mother was mugged."

"It didn't come up." Lorry shrugged and turned toward her mother. "Is everything inside?"

"Yes." Pat nodded. "Everything!"

"That was lucky," Lorry told her. "Who was the man that retrieved your purse?"

"Do you remember Brand Goddard?" Pat asked.

"Yes, he's one of Tammy's teachers," Lorry answered.

"Wasn't he also one of Ashley's crushes when she was in high school?" Pat frowned, trying to remember which one of her younger daughters it was.

"No, I think it was Hannah who had a crush on him," Lorry corrected her. "He was also one the people who bullied her or let his snooty girlfriend bully Hannah."

"Oh, that's right!" Pat nodded before patting her purse. "Well, he's a hero to me today."

"I'll remember to thank him the next time he calls me to discuss Tammy's science grades." Lorry wasn't about to be fooled by one good deed from Brand Goddard.

The man hadn't been very nice to three of her sisters when he was at school and didn't have a good reputation from his sports star days either. Brand also had the reputation of being a ladies' man whose ex-wife died under mysterious circumstances.

"Lorry!" Pat rolled her eyes at her eldest daughter. "You need to learn how to forgive people, my dear, and learn that while a leopard may not be able to change its spots, they can fade over time."

"Yes, but the spots are still there." Lorry gave her mother a smug smile.

"I don't see your car," Tom changed the subject as he glanced around the parking area.

"It's at my—" Pat didn't get to finish her sentence when Lorry butted in.

"I think my mother left her car at your father's house!" Lorry drawled, folding her arms and seeing the surprise in her mother's eyes that Lorry knew.

"Oh!" Tom's eyebrows shot up in surprise, making Lorry realize he hadn't known about the relationship. He cleared his throat and recovered from his shock quickly. "Can I give you a lift back to your car?"

"No, it's okay," Pat told him. "Now that I have my keys and don't need my spare, I'm sure Margorie can give me a lift."

"Do you need to go to the doctor?" Tom asked her.

"No, I'm fine. I didn't get hurt," Pat assured her. "But thank you for asking."

"Are you sure you're okay?" Tom's eyes scanned Pat.

"I agree with Tom that we should take you to get checked out by a doctor," Lorry told her. "You said you had a fall."

"It's just a little bruising." Pat waved them off with a soft laugh. "Now get back to work, the two of you. I know how busy you both are, and I'm sorry to have caused you both distress."

Lorry didn't get a chance to reply. Pat's face turned ashen. Her brow creased into a frown as she started to sway before her eyes closed, and she began to crumple to the floor.

"MOM!" Lorry shouted.

Before Lorry could reach out to grab Pat, Tom had stepped toward her and grabbed her before she hit the ground.

AVAILABLE ON **AMAZON**

SCOTT SISTERS SERIES

Series Books:

<u>The Beach Hotel on Marco Island</u> – Prequel

<u>The Bookstore on Marco Island</u> – Book 1

<u>The Baby on Marco Island</u> – Book 2

<u>The Bachelor on Marco Island</u> – Book 3

<u>The Restuarant on Marco Island</u> – Book 4

<u>The Studio on Marco Island</u> – Book 5

<u>The Bride on Marco Island</u> – Book 6

AVAILABLE ON **AMAZON**

ALSO FROM AMY RAFFERTY

SWEET COLORADO ROMANCE

CHRISTMAS AT MISTLETOE LODGE – BOOK 1

"Walking away from you, leaving you standing there at the altar… it tore me apart. But I thought it was the right thing to do."

Avery Hawthorne left behind a lot when she moved to California.

Her family, the familiarity—and a small-town romance with an enigmatic ex she's tried to forget.

As the holidays roll around, she's determined to earn a promotion from her boss and make the sacrifices all worth it.

But this new task means going back to the place she fled twelve years ago.

Her boss is confident the deal for Mistletoe Lodge will be easy. The owners are drowning in debt and Avery has 'history' with the Carlisle family. What he doesn't know is that her history with them is anything but good.

Avery's ex, Ryder Carlisle, is determined to keep his family's inn afloat and has ideas to revamp it. The last thing he wants is to give in to some big corporate hotel chain. But he never imagined they'd send the one person he couldn't say "no" to!

Avery just wants to celebrate Christmas with a promotion.

Ryder wants to keep Mistletoe Lodge in the family.

In a battle of wills over Christmas festivities, Avery and Ryder reignite old flames as they wrestle with their wills—and their own feelings, which remain just as strong twelve years later.

It was official. Fate really had hijacked her festive season and was busy toying with her...

CHRISTMAS AT MISTLETOE LODGE is Book 1 of the Feel Good Holiday Romance series, a powerful women's fiction saga in which Avery and Ryder have a second chance at romance if they can push aside their stubbornness and the wrongs of the past...

AVAILABLE ON **AMAZON**

COMING SOON FROM AMY RAFFERTY

COBBLE BEACH ROMANCE SERIES - BOOK 1

THE LIGHTHOUSE ON PLUM ISLAND

CHAPTER 1

Caroline Shaw's heart raced with exhilaration after her meeting with Travis Danes. As she strolled through the bustling streets of New York alongside her lifelong friend, Jennifer Gains, palpable excitement filled the air. Travis had wholeheartedly agreed to her terms, and within three to six months, a film crew would descend on Plum Island to bring her beloved "Cobble Cove Mysteries" to life on screen. It was a dream unfolding before her eyes.

"Can you believe it, Jen?" Caroline gushed, her hazel eyes sparkling with joy. "He actually agreed to everything! The film crew will be on Plum Island soon, and we'll be making magic together!"

Jennifer, who had been Caroline's unwavering source of support since childhood, beamed in response. "I always knew you could do it, Caroline. Your writing is brilliant, and now the world will not only read your work but see it come to life."

Their destination was Jennifer's favorite coffee shop in Soho, a haven of creativity and conversation. Just as they arrived at the charming spot, Jennifer's phone rang, and she sighed regretfully.

"It's work," Jennifer said apologetically. "I'm so sorry, Caroline. I have to take this."

"No worries," Caroline replied with a reassuring smile. They were close to the cafe entrance, and she gestured for Jennifer to go ahead. "I'll have a coffee and write while you handle business. We can catch up later at your place for our celebration dinner."

Jennifer made sure the owner of the coffee shop noticed them and guided Caroline to her usual table by the window before rushing off to attend to her call. Caroline settled into her seat, and Simon Newbury, the cafe's owner, greeted them warmly.

"Good afternoon, ladies," Simon said with a charming smile. "You both look lovely today."

"Thank you, Simon," they chimed in unison, and Caroline took a menu.

"Why are you still standing?" Simon inquired with a quizzical look at Jennifer.

"Because I have to get back to work," Jennifer groaned, and then she added, "Please put Caroline's order on my tab."

"You don't have to do that," Caroline protested.

She felt her cheeks flush as she accepted Jennifer's offer. The cafe's prices were exorbitant, and even though Simon's coffee and treats were top-notch, they didn't warrant such costs.

"Nonsense," Jennifer insisted. "Consider it my treat. Besides, consider it a business expense, with you being my top client."

Simon turned to Caroline. "Can I get you your usual coffee while you peruse the menu?"

"Yes, please, Simon," Caroline replied with gratitude. Simon nodded and excused himself to fulfill their orders.

"I'd better get going," Jennifer said, her tone apologetic. "I'll see you back at my place this evening."

Caroline bid her friend farewell and Jennifer left the cafe, disappearing into the bustling city. As Caroline settled in, her coffee arrived, and she decided to forgo any food and instead set up her laptop. The cafe's creative ambiance was infectious, and she was eager to dive back into her writing.

With her laptop screen glowing before her, Caroline's thoughts drifted back over the past three years. Her father had passed away from a heart attack just two months before she'd discovered her husband, Robert Parker, was cheating on her. Two weeks after that revelation, she lost her job as the head of NYU Libraries.

Robert had insisted on keeping their house, a brownstone on the Upper West Side of New York, leaving Caroline and their twelve-year-old daughter, Jules, with nowhere to go. Jennifer had graciously taken them in, and they had lived in her three-bedroom Soho apartment for nearly six months, depleting Caroline's meager savings as she desperately searched for new employment.

However, there weren't many opportunities for a forty-four-year-old librarian in New York City. During Jules's school hours and between interviews, Caroline had begun writing "Cobble Cove Mysteries." Writing had become her refuge, a way to escape her shattered marriage, fading career, and the resentment of her now fourteen-year-old daughter.

Jules had been furious when Caroline uprooted their lives and moved them back to Plum Island, her small hometown in New England. She held Caroline responsible for the divorce and blamed her for everything that had gone wrong. However, their bond had recently started to mend as they collaborated on Caroline's new book, and the prospect of the TV series had brought them closer.

Caroline sighed contentedly and turned her attention back to her writing, eager to immerse herself in the world of her characters once more. However, her solitude was short-lived as a tall, impeccably dressed man approached her table. He appeared slightly flustered but politely asked if he could share her table.

Caroline surveyed the crowded cafe and realized that every seat was taken. She offered a friendly smile and gestured to the empty chair. "Of course, please have a seat."

The man smiled gratefully and settled into the chair across from her. He seemed like a creature from a different world, with his expensive attire and an air of sophistication that contrasted sharply with the cafe's casual atmosphere.

A server promptly arrived at their table, and the man ordered a sugary designer coffee concoction, which didn't take long to arrive. Caroline couldn't help but suppress a shudder at the sweetness overload. The man seemed to notice her reaction and chuckled as he took a sip.

"I have a sweet tooth," he confessed, striking up a conversation. "My parents are always on my case about it. Even my sixteen-year-old son shakes his head at me when I have to satisfy my sugar cravings."

"My teenage daughter has a sweet tooth, too," Caroline mused.

"Really?" He chuckled. "Teenagers and their sweet tooth! It's a universal struggle, it seems." He held out his hand. "I'm Brad."

"Caroline." She shook his hand and noticed his handshake was firm but not rough.

As Caroline sipped her coffee, she soon found herself engaged in a pleasant conversation with Brad. While they chatted, Caroline couldn't help but observe him discreetly. Brad was a striking figure. She estimated his height to be roughly six foot three inches, just like her brother. His stylish, short, straight, jet-black hair was graced with subtle streaks of gray at the temples, framing a strong and handsome face that looked like a great artist chiseled it. Brad's piercing blue eyes sparkled with a warmth that drew you in, and when he smiled, it was nothing short of heart-stopping.

Their discussion meandered from favorite books to travel destinations, and Caroline found herself genuinely enjoying Brad's company. It was a rarity for her to strike up conversations with strangers, especially a strange man. Caroline learned that he was from New York, but his job in the entertainment industry took him all over the world. He had a sixteen-year-old son, Connor, who was his pride and joy. The two of them had been close since his wife left them when Connor was eight months old. Except for a few visits, Connor didn't know his mother well, and he shied away from what he did know.

"I'm thankful that my son and I have such a close bond," Brad told her. "I always worried when I was younger that my kids wouldn't be as close to me as I was with my parents."

"Are your parents still around?" Caroline asked.

"Yes, my mother and father are still both fit and don't look a day older than fifty-five." Brad laughed. "Or so my mother likes to tell everyone."

"I was close to my parents, too," Caroline admitted.

"By was, you mean—" Brad's brows crinkled as he looked at her questioningly.

"My mother passed away ten years ago from cancer." Caroline swallowed the burning lump, thinking about her mother still brought to her throat. She cleared her throat. "My father passed away three years ago from a heart attack."

"I'm sorry." Brad's eyes filled with compassion. "Do you have siblings?"

"Yes, I have an older brother. He also lives in New England," Caroline told him. "Well, he's actually my half-brother. His mother passed away during childbirth."

"Oh, no, that's horrible," Brad said.

"My mother was a doctor at the hospital in Boston where my brother was born," Caroline explained. "His mother had a complicated pregnancy and had been hospitalized for her last two months."

"How did your parents end up getting together?" Brad's brows tightened in a curious frown.

"A year later, my father took my brother to the hospital because he was having breathing problems and was sent to a specialist at Boston General, where my mother worked." Caroline had no idea why she was blurting out her family history to a complete stranger, but Brad seemed genuinely interested. "They ran into each other again, and as my brother had to stay in hospital for tests for nearly two months, they saw each other daily." She smiled, thinking about the story her father told her. "One thing led to another, and they fell in love. My mother fell in love with the small town where my father lived and started a small practice on the island."

"You never wanted to become a doctor?" Brad frowned.

"Oh, no." Caroline's eyes widened. "I can't stand the sight of blood." She shuddered. "I was always more of a bookworm who loved to read. All I ever wanted to do was lose myself in stories."

"That's why you became a librarian." Brad smiled and sat back in the chair. "I'm glad libraries still exist with the internet being around."

"They do, but sadly, most of the books are being overlooked for the computers libraries have now." Caroline sighed. "I've just realized my life may seem such a bore compared to your jet-setting one."

"My life is tiring, and between you and me," Brad leaned forward and lowered his voice, "I'm actually afraid of flying."

"Oh, me too." Caroline nodded, wide-eyed. "I'm nervous while in the air, but I think the worst parts are the—"

"Take-off and landing," they said in unison and laughed.

"You know, I've always wanted to visit New England," Brad admitted. "The historic towns and the coastal beauty all sound incredibly charming."

"I can't believe you've been nearly everywhere there is to go in the United States, the world, and you've never been to New England." Caroline's eyes lit up as she spoke about her hometown. "It's a wonderful place. Although I spent most of my adult and married life in New York, my heart was still firmly planted in New England."

"Well, it's true," Brad assured her. "I've skirted around the area." He leaned back in his chair, a thoughtful expression on his face. "But hearing you talk about it and seeing how your eyes light up when you explain it, I'm definitely going to make an effort to get there."

Their conversation continued to flow effortlessly, touching on a myriad of topics. As the minutes turned into hours, Caroline found herself captivated by the man and surprised by the connection they were forming. It was a rare and unexpected pleasure, and she couldn't deny the sense of warmth that had enveloped her during their conversation.

The bustling coffee shop around them seemed to fade into the background as they shared stories and laughter. Time flew by, and Caroline couldn't help but feel a pang of disappointment when she realized how late it had gotten. She glanced at her wristwatch and then back at Brad.

"I should probably be heading back soon," Caroline said reluctantly. "The friend I'm staying with while I'm in New York will be waiting for me, and I have to check in with my daughter, who's staying with her father while we're in New York."

Brad nodded, a hint of regret in his eyes. "Of course. It's been a pleasure getting to know you."

Caroline gathered her things and stood up, and Brad stood with her. Her heart was heavy with the knowledge that she would have to say goodbye. But as she prepared to leave, Brad surprised her by extending an invitation.

"I know this is sudden, but would you like to join me for dinner tomorrow night?" Brad asked, his eyes filled with sincerity. "I'd love to continue our conversation."

Caroline hesitated for a moment, her mind racing. She barely knew Brad, and yet there was an undeniable connection between them. With a smile, she decided to take a leap of faith.

"I'd like that," she replied, her heart pounding with anticipation.

"Why don't we meet back here tomorrow evening around six?" Brad suggested.

"That sounds like a plan," Caroline said, hoping he couldn't hear how heavily her heart thudded against her rib cage. "Until tomorrow, then."

Brad raised her hand to his lips, gently kissing her knuckles. "Until tomorrow, Caroline."

Brad's smile was heart-stopping, and Caroline had to force her knees not to buckle under its impact. She gave herself a mental shake and gathered all her strength to walk out of the coffee shop without him seeing her jelly legs or collapsing in a puddle of mushy goo.

As she made her way to Jennifer's apartment, her mind was filled with images of Brad and how she'd had her first serendipitous moment. Caroline's footsteps echoed down the quiet corridor as she approached Jennifer's apartment. She couldn't shake the excitement from her chance encounter with him, the intriguing stranger who had entered her life so unexpectedly. Thoughts of their upcoming dinner date warmed her heart, and she couldn't wait to share the details with Jennifer.

As she reached Jennifer's door, Caroline fumbled for her keys, eager to get inside, but the door flew open before she could open it. Her anticipation turned to concern when she noticed Jennifer staring at her with an expression of a mixture of relief and worry.

"Caroline!" Jennifer exclaimed, her voice edged with worry as she grabbed Caroline and hugged her before pushing her away to look at her. "Where have you been? I've been trying to call you for ages. I was about to phone the police!"

Caroline checked her phone and was shocked to find a barrage of missed calls and messages from both Jennifer and Jules. She had been so engrossed in her conversation with Brad that she hadn't noticed her phone buzzing in her bag.

"I'm so sorry, Jen," Caroline apologized, feeling guilty for causing her friend so much distress. "I lost track of time. Let me check in with Jules. She's also been messaging."

Jennifer nodded, her concern easing. She stepped aside for Caroline to enter. Caroline dialed her daughter's number as she walked inside. Jules answered after the third ring. Before Caroline had finished greeting her daughter, she learned that Jules was upset because her father and his new wife were planning to convert her childhood bedroom into a nursery for their expected baby. Caroline did her best to placate her daughter, promising to talk to her father about finding a solution.

Once she hung up, Caroline hurriedly got ready, feeling a sense of urgency to make amends for her absence. Jennifer, who had been patient throughout, smiled as she saw Caroline's anxiousness.

"Don't worry," Jennifer reassured her. "We still have time to make our reservation at 'Le Petit Lueur.' It's one of the finest restaurants in Soho, and I'm sure you'll love it."

"I'm sure I will," Caroline said. "You know how much I love French cuisine."

Forty minutes later, they made their way to the restaurant. It was a hidden gem nestled in the heart of Soho. Its exterior was unassuming, but they were greeted by a warm, intimate atmosphere as they stepped inside. Soft candlelight flickered on white linen-covered tables, casting a romantic glow. The aroma of exquisite dishes filled the air, and the gentle hum of conversation added to the restaurant's charm.

Over a sumptuous meal, Caroline explained why she'd been so late returning to Jennifer's apartment. She shared the story of her chance meeting with Brad and how she'd agreed to go on a dinner date with him.

"Caroline, I can't believe you, of all people, agreed to go on a dinner date with a complete stranger!" Jennifer stared at her in disbelief.

"We spoke for hours," Caroline reminded her. "So, we're technically not strangers anymore."

"It is good to see you so perky and dreamy again." Jennifer smiled. "Maybe a New York fling will be good for you."

Caroline couldn't help but smile at her friend's openness to new possibilities. She agreed to download a tracking app on her phone, allowing Jennifer to keep an eye on her during the date, which put Jennifer's mind at ease.

As they finished their meal and took a leisurely stroll back to Jennifer's apartment, Jennifer finally revealed the reason behind her rushed meeting earlier in the day. Her voice carried a hint of sadness as she spoke.

"The truth is, the publishing house isn't doing well," Jennifer confessed. "They've decided to downsize, and I'm one of the people being laid off. In six months, I'll be unemployed."

Caroline's heart ached for her friend, knowing how much Jennifer had dedicated herself to her career in publishing. But she also saw an opportunity, a chance to inspire Jennifer to follow her own dreams as she'd done for Caroline.

Taking a deep breath, Caroline stopped walking and faced Jennifer. "Jen, I know this is a difficult time, but it might also be a chance for you to pursue what you've always wanted."

Jennifer looked puzzled, and Caroline continued, her voice filled with conviction.

"Remember how you've always wanted to open your own Entertainment Management firm? Publishing was supposed to be a stopgap until you could afford to do it. Maybe now is the time."

Jennifer's eyes widened as Caroline's words sank in. She had indeed dreamed of running her own company, guiding talent in the entertainment industry, and shaping careers. But life, with its demands and responsibilities, had pushed that dream aside.

Caroline placed a reassuring hand on Jennifer's shoulder. "Jennifer, this setback could be the universe's way of telling you it's time to follow your passion. It's never too late to chase your dreams, my friend."

She smiled. "Isn't that what you told me not too long ago? And look, I've got a book deal for my series and a television series."

Jennifer's face slowly lit up with hope and determination. "You know what? Maybe you're right. Perhaps it's time I took that leap of faith."

They continued their stroll. Caroline could see the weight of uncertainty lift from Jennifer's shoulders. As they walked together under the city's glittering skyline, Caroline couldn't help but feel that life had a way of weaving unexpected threads into their stories, leading them toward brighter tomorrows.

AVAILABLE ON **AMAZON**

MORE BOOKS BY AMY RAFFERTY

SERIES

Christmas at Mistletoe Lodge ~ *A Feel Good Holiday Romance*

New Year at Mistletoe Lodge ~ *A Feel Good Holiday Romance*

Reunion at Mistletoe Lodge ~ *A Feel Good Holiday Romance*

The Bakery in Bar Harbor ~ *Secrets in Maine Series*

Cupids Bow Ranch ~ *Montana Country Inn Romance Series*

Starting Over in Nantucket ~ *Cody Bay Inn Series*

Leave a Rose in the Sand ~ *Starting Over in Key West Series*

A Mystery at Summer Lodge ~ *A Coastal Vineyard Series*

Charming Bookshop Mysteries ~ *Small Town Beach Romance*

Moonlight Dream ~ *Honey Bay Cafe Series*

Nantucket Christmas Escape ~ *Second Chance Holiday Romance*

Retreat ~ *Manatee Bay Series*

Secrets of White Sands Cove ~ *A San Diego Sunset Series*

The Seabreeze Cottage ~ *La Jolla Cove Series*

STANDALONE NOVELS

The McCaid Sisters ~ *A Second Chance Romance Mystery Novel*

BOX SETS

Montana Country Inn: The Complete Collection ~ *Montana Country Inn Romance Series*

Cody Bay Inn: The Complete Collection ~ *Nantucket Romance Series*

Starting Over in Key West: The Complete Collection ~ *A Florida Keys Romance Series*

A Mystery at Summer Lodge: The Complete Collection ~ *A Coastal Vineyard Series*

Charming Bookshop Mysteries: The Complete Collection ~ *Small Town Beach Romance*

Honey Bay Cafe Series: The Complete Collection ~ *Second Chance Beach Mystery Romance*

Nantucket Christmas Escape: The Complete Collection ~ *Second Chance Holiday Romance*

Manatee Bay: The Complete Collection ~ *Treasure Seekers Beach Romance Series*

Secrets of White Sands Cove: The Complete Collection ~ *A San Diego Sunset Series*

The Seabreeze Cottage: The Complete Collection ~ *La Jolla Cove Series*

THREE IN ONE

Coastal Collection: Sea Breeze Cottage, Mystery at Summer Lodge, Secrets of White Sands Cove ~ *Three Series in One Book*

SPANISH VERSION

El Café de Bahía Honey ~ *Honey Bay Cafe (Spanish)*

Escapada Navideña a Nantucket ~ *Nantucket Christmas Escape (Spanish)*

Bahía de Manatee ~ *Manatee Bay (Spanish)*

La Posada de la Bahía Cody – *Cody Bay Inn (Spanish)*

AMY RAFFERTY VIP READERS

Don't want to miss out on my giveaways, competitions,

and 'hot off the press' news?

Subscribe to my email list.

It is FREE!

Click Here!

CONNECT WITH AMY RAFFERTY

Not only can you check out the latest news and deals there,

you can also get an email alert each time I release my next book.

Follow me on BookBub

I always love to hear from you and get your feedback.

Email me at ~ books@amyraffertyauthor.com

Follow on Amazon ~ Amy Rafferty

Sign up for my newsletter and free gift, Here

Join my 'Amy's Friends' group on Facebook

CONNECT WITH ROSE RYAN

Sign up for my newsletter and keep up on all the latest book news,

release dates,

excerpts, monthly giveaways, and more!

Or follow me on my other socials including:

Facebook , **Instagram**, **Bookbub** , and **Goodreads**

Follow my author central page on Amazon: **Rose Ryan:**

A NOTE FROM AMY RAFFERTY

Hi, wonderful people,

Having been described as "The Queen of Gorgeous Clean Mystery Romance," I am delighted that you are here.

I write sweet women's romance fiction for ages 20 and upwards. I bring you heartwarming, page-turning fiction featuring unforgettable families and friends and the ups and downs they face.

My mission is to bring you beach reads and feel-good fiction that fills your heart with emotion and love. You will find comfort in my strong female lead role models, along with the men who love them. Fill your hearts with family saga, the power of friendship, second chances, and later-in-life romance.

I write books you cannot put down, bringing sunshine to your days and nights.

Thank you for being here and reading my books x

A NOTE FROM ROSE RYAN

Hi, incredible people,

I love writing women's romance novels that are sweet, filled with mystery plots, heartfelt emotions, family drama and second chances.

I welcome you to join me on this exciting adventure of writing heart-warming contemporary beach romance novels.

Also, it would mean the world to me if you would kindly leave a review on my stories using the link below which takes you to my author page on Amazon.

I appreciate you all.

I hope my writing brings happiness and inspiration to you!

Thanks for being here!

Rose x

*It would mean a lot to me if you would be so kind and leave me an honest review for **The Baby on Marco Island**.*

The link I have placed below makes it so easy as it is a special link taking you straight to the review section.

Thank you in advance and I appreciate you.

Amazon.com/review/create-review?&asin=B0CKFPBF5P

Made in the USA
Middletown, DE
30 August 2024